The Angel and the Sphinx

The Angel and the Sphinx

by
Edouard Schuré

Translated, annotated and introduced by
Brian Stableford

A Black Coat Press Book

Visit our website at www.blackcoatpress.com

ISBN 978-1-61227-879-7. First Printing: August 2019. Published by Black Coat Press, an imprint of Hollywood Comics.com, LLC, P.O. Box 17270, Encino, CA 91416. All rights reserved.

TABLE OF CONTENTS

Introduction

L'Ange et la sphinge by Édouard Schuré, here
translated as *The Angel and the Sphinx*, was first published in 1897 by Perrin et Cie, on behalf of the Librairie
Académique Didier. It was the author's first novel. The
story included with it in this volume as a makeweight,
"L'Élève du Tintoret," here translated as "Tintoretto's
Pupil," which might have been Schuré's first published
work of prose fiction, appeared in the 1 September 1882
issue of *La Nouvelle Revue*.

Édouard Schuré (1841-1929) was a prolific writer
of non-fiction, mostly about music and literature, and he
was a regular contributor to the *Revue des Deux Mondes*
from the 1870s onwards, but his fiction is relatively
sparse, although he wrote poetry and dramatic works in
the early part of his career. The novel translated herein
was followed rapidly by his second, *Le Double*, serial-
ized in *La Nouvelle Revue* in 1898 and reprinted as a
book a year later. Schuré is best known today as the author of *Les Grand Initiés* (1889; tr. as *The Great Initi-
ates*), a series of studies of the key figures in the so-
called Hermetic Tradition of great magicians and mys-
tics, which became one of the bestselling works of the
French Occult Revival and a standard work of scholarly
fantasy.

Born in Strasbourg and bilingual in German and
French, Schuré completed his formal education at the
University of Strasbourg, graduating in law, but never
practiced, preferring to dedicate himself to scholarship,

initially focusing on the history of German folk music and literature and the relationship between German Romanticism and idealist philosophy. His first scholarly work was a massive *Histoire du lied, ou La Chanson populaire en Allemagne* (1868). The intersection of his scholarly interests inevitably led him to pay close attention to the work of Richard Wagner, on whom he wrote a major study, *Richard Wagner et le drame musical* (1875), and for whom he became an ardent propagandist, forming a close friendship with the composer.

Schuré was a member of the French contingent invited to attend the first performance of *Die Walküre*, which took place at the Königliches Hof-und National Theater in Munich on 26 June 1870, at the insistence of Wagner's patron, Ludwig II of Bavaria. The other French writers in the party included Catulle Mendès, Auguste Villiers de l'Isle-Adam and Mendès wife, Judith—Théophile Gautier's daughter, who subsequently reverted to signing her work with her maiden name—although the two had already separated; the composers Camille Saint-Saëns and Henri Duparc were also in the group. Twenty years later, Mendès published a remarkable short story in the *Écho de Paris*, of which he was then the literary editor, "Un Village, près de la route..." (tr. as "A Village near the Road") in which the members of the party—all easily identifiable, although only Villiers is named—are subjected to a strange supernatural experience after the performance, a story that Mendès' acquaintance with Schuré might well have influenced.

That event in Munich was rapidly followed by the Franco-Prussian War, which forced Schuré to decide exactly where his cultural and political allegiance lay, and he made a strong commitment to France, although he maintained his relationship with Wagner, and met

Friedrich Nietzsche though him, who became another significant influence on his thinking. Under the influence of the esoteric scholar Antoine Fabre d'Olivet, Schuré became increasing interested in occultism, and in the 1880s, he became an important figure in the French Occult Revival, culminating in the publication of *Les Grand Initiés*. The most successful of his other works was his oft-reprinted study of *Les Grandes légendes de France* (1892), in which he made much of the "Celtic genius" of Bretagne, adding fuel to a current vogue dubbed "Celtomania" by its detractors—a fascination that eventually culminated in his analysis of *L'Âme celtique et le génie de la France à travers les âges* (1921). After a brief flirtation with theosophy in the 1890s, Schuré formed a close association in the early years of the twentieth century with the breakaway theosophist Rudolf Steiner, one of whose French translators he became, and whose philosophical dramas he influenced.

L'Ange et la sphinge, like much fiction by writers associated with the Occult Revival, is a Symbolist novel, and it has close associations with the contemporary work of Gilbert-Augustin Thierry, also a regular contributor to the *Revue des Deux Mondes*. Thierry was similarly interested in the themes of reincarnation and expiation, and was also fascinated by the allegedly baleful role of physical Amour in human affairs. *L'Ange et la sphinge* is by no means the most sophisticated of the many accounts of exotic *femmes fatales* produced in French literature by members of the Romantic and Symbolist Movements, but it is one of the most graphic and one of the most intense. It is notable that it recycles the symbolic apparatus deployed in "L'Éleve du Tintoret," but the imagery of the siren deployed metaphorically in the earlier story becomes more nearly literal in the novel; the latter does not shirk its fantastic apparatus and does not hesitate to hybridize it, conflating the siren with the sphinx and adding further imagery in the interests of decoration, making the story one of the most phantasmagorical of its era.

Only one of Schuré's novels has been previously translated into English, *La Prêtresse d'Isis, légende de Pompei* (1907; tr. as *The Priestess of Isis*), which is almost exactly contemporary with Gilbert-Augustin Thierry's *La Fresque de Pompei* ((1907; tr. as "The Pompeian Fresco"), a work that shows the marked influence of Schuré, and recycles some of the imagery of *L'Ange et the sphinge. La Prêtresse d'Isis* is not Schuré's best novel, however, and suffers somewhat in comparison with both *L'Ange et la sphinge* and the Thierry novel similarly inspired by the excavations at Pompeii. *Le Double*, which is a contemporary novel, is certainly interesting in its particular deployment of the *femme fatale* theme, but its careful ambiguity is not necessarily to its advantage when compared with the bold flamboyance of *L'Ange et la sphinge*. Aficionados of fantasy fiction will unhesitatingly prefer *L'Ange et la sphinge* to any of the author's other works of fiction, and connoisseurs of Symbolist fiction will also find abundant reward therein to make up for its blithe lack of subtlety. The novel is, in essence, a *jeu d'esprit*, rejoicing in its freedom from the scholarly restraint the author felt obliged to retain in the bulk of his work, and that exuberance enables the story to remain very enjoyable today.

The translation of *L'Ange et la sphinge* was made from the London Library's copy of the Perrin edition. The translation of "L'Éleve du Tintoret" was made from the copy of the relevant volume of *La Nouvelle Revue* reproduced on the Bibliothèque Nationale's *gallica* web-site.

Brian Stableford

THE ANGEL AND THE SPHINX

At the foot of the deserted castle the weary knight
went to sleep. At midnight he went up into the
illuminated hall. Next to the blazing hearth, an
unknown bride was waiting.
She was weaving a crown of myrtle in her
dark tresses and her gaze was a gaze of
eternity...
Their eyes met; they were exchanged rings
when the cock suddenly crowed.
She paled like a phantom; everything
vanished in a gray dawn...and the knight
woke up.
The Legend of the Black Forest.

From a German Manuscript of the Sixteenth Century

Am I truly a monk, a tonsured monk in the silence
of the cloister, me, Konrad von Felseneck, the free
knight? I once had a castle perched on a mountain; at my
feet, dense forests in which deer were abundant, profound valleys with fresh mills, handsome squires and
gray falcons. I had all that... And now, the bare walls of
a cell, the black crucifix, and, behind my grilled window, the great elms of the brothers' covered walk, are all
that remain to me.

But Lord God, could I do otherwise? Am I not
criminal, perhaps less criminal than mad, the victim of a

malediction come from afar...yes, from before me...from another self...from sins accumulated in my other existence...as Master Rupertus said?

What is there in my life that is true? Feasts, tourneys, hunts, war cries and cajoling women's voices have all fled. No, nothing was true. They were shadows, nothing but shadows. Life in decline is like water running over dead leaves, the laughter of the wind that glides through the thickets and has already gone when one talks about it.

Something was real, however, terribly real, in my evil life: something ineffaceable. Two images remain to me, two indestructible memories. They are there, between me and the blank wall of my cell; they accompany me over the funereal paving stones of the cloister. They come back, above all, when I sing the office with the brothers in the apse, beneath the tenebrous arch of the choir, where the eternal lamp hangs. From the height of the vault they gaze at me, the two women who made my destiny and who are still disputing the shreds of my agonizing heart.

She is still there, the Unique, the Unforgettable, the Fiancée of the Dream, the Shade, impalpable and distant, but so real and so present that all the women of flesh have been unable to efface the imprint. How pale she is beneath her bridal veil! How profound her gaze is! It is a gaze of eternity...

And the other is also there, alas: the Sphinx-Woman, the subtle and carnal monster that has burned my nights and devastated my days. Begone, accursed! But no; she arches her white torso; her breasts are erect; she twists her neck and laughs malevolently... Disappear, or I shall strike!

Oh, who can decipher the unfathomable enigma of those two ever-present images, in which my entire life is concentrated? By virtue of seeing them, my cheeks have become hollow and the flesh has melted over my bones; and, young as yet in years, I am already old.

What do I hear? The light trills of the nightingale suspended in its cage, in front of the prior's cell. Poor captive, its voice becomes sad with the falling dusk. It hurls its long, dolorous notes into the night...

Oh, the folly of song, amour and life!

Before dying or losing my reason, let us write down the memories that obsess me.

I. The Virgin of the Stained-Glass Window

I see myself, as a child twelve years old, perched on the highest tower of the castle, which stands on a wooded summit of the Black Forest, overlooking a vast extent of mountains and the entire valley of the Rhine. At my feet is the heavy building with the tangled roofs, the walls bristling with crenellations and slender turrets. On the square terrace of the keep, which serves as my vantage point, stands a large pole, on which a yellow banner floats, armoried with a black griffin. The flag announces the presence in the castle of my father, Graf von Felseneck. By my side, my master-of-arms, the old squire Siegwart with the harsh features and a steely gaze, tugs the cord that retains the banner, brings it down and rolls it up; for the lord is going away.

From the interior courtyard, as deep as a well, confused sounds rise: the whinnying of horses, the clink of arms, rude human voices. My father, with thirty vassals, is going to join the Elector, who is accompanying the Emperor to the war. The troop has already crossed the drawbridge. The sentry salutes them with a blast of the trumpet, to which the men-at-arms respond: "Hurrah! Hurrah!"

Now the file of horsemen descends the path that snakes around the base of the huge castle and then plunges into the forest. It appears again in a clearing; I see helmets glistening in the sunlight; finally, it disappears under the trees.

Then I too utter a cry of joy into the blue sky, a cry of deliverance that causes Siegwart to say: "Silence, little wild falcon, or I'll shut you in your cage—you know, the dark armory where the evil black panoplies are."

But old Siegwart doesn't scare me, in spite of his terrible eyes. I stroke his white and yellow beard, which resembles the moss of fir-trees torn by the wind.

"Tomorrow," I say to him, "we'll go hunting, a long, long way. And when I'm grown up, I'll give you a fine fief..."

"A fief? What would I do with it? But if you don't learn to handle the sword and the lance, you'll never be a knight."

Siegwart, bending down, grunting, opens the trap-door with his arm of iron and descends the staircase into the tower. I remain on the terrace. With my father gone, I feel that I have become the monarch of the country. The thousand arrows of the fir-trees that are mounting an assault toward me from abyssal depths, the kite that is soaring overhead, and the silver clouds murmur: "You're free!"

I see the dense forests undulate, blurred by light, and the green plain dissolving at the horizon. Then my heart swells and responds to things: "Yes, the world belongs to me!"

I have not conserved any memory of my mother. I was scarcely two years old when she died. My father only made rare appearances at the castle. His life was spent far away, at the Elector's court or at war. I grew up thus, like an orphan, in the vast castle, with my two masters, the good chaplain and squire Siegwart.

As far as my memory goes back, I led two lives: that of the castle and that outside; one of meditation and dream, plunged in study and books, the other of movement and action, spread out in the open air, dispersed in the woods. For a long time, those two existences ran parallel within me, like two rivers of different hues, which were juxtaposed without mingling. Delivered to one, I absorbed myself within it passionately and forgot the other, until the moment when it gripped me entirely again.

Oh, the long hours spent listening to the interminable stories that the chaplain told me, or reading romances of chivalry, to the sway of the linden trees in the double arch of the window—how lightly and diaphanously they passed, and how I savored them! And I loved no less riding with Siegwart beneath the spring foliage, and the barking of dogs over the snow in the forest sparkling with frost. In the free days of twelve to fifteen years of age, they were the sole joys of my life. I was unaware of the world, but I possessed myself without knowing myself, in an interior and inexpressible dream.

And yet, strange impressions were already disquieting me then; I saw looming up before me the painful enigma, the undecipherable enigma, of existence.

In the castle of Felseneck there is one place that inspired me from early childhood with an ardent curiosity and a superstitious dread. I mean the chapel that my mother had had constructed, in the year of my birth and her death, by a young master of Nuremberg, equally renowned as an architect and as a painter on glass. It was the only living memory of my mother, a monument to her vanished soul, so I adored it.

From one of the interior courtyards one penetrates into a little nave of bare gray granite. To the left there is a sarcophagus in a niche. The upper part represents my mother, supine, her hands joined over her breast, a greyhound curled up at her feet. At the back is a stone Christ; one can scarcely see the two arms of the cross and the body of the Savior in the penumbra. The marvel of the place is a brace of ogival windows ornamented with stained glass. They are flamboyant against the blackness of the walls and cast a supernatural gaze into the darkness of the sanctuary.

The window to the right represents a svelte virgin in a crimson robe, her pale face raised to the sky, her eyes ecstatic. The nimbus of her hair flows from her head over her shoulders like a river ablaze with amour. Her luminous feet, martyrized feet speckled with drops of blood, are trampling a cloud where an impotent chimera is writhing. The saint is holding a red tulip in her left hand, from which flames are escaping, and a palm of victory in her right hand. Behind her, the celestial Jerusalem is staged beneath the azure sky, like a white fortress.

Facing the triumphant virgin, another ogival stained glass window shines. It depicts a knight in bright armor standing in a leafy forest. He is holding a beautiful horse by the bridle, which has an almost human gaze, seemingly scenting combat with its flared nostrils, and whinnying at the fanfare. The face of the knight, beneath his raised visor, framed by the helm and gorgerin, is sad but resolute. Around him, in the forest, an entire population of demons, monsters and sinister larvae is climbing and sniggering. They are emerging from the roots, swarming over the branches, extending their claws, their wing-cases and their hairy wings toward the warrior, widening their rapacious eyes over him. But the knight does not see them. His firm and cold gaze is contemplating a distant bloody battle before hurling himself into it, while his iron-gloved fist restrains the superb horse by the shaggy mane.

With what spell had the unknown master infused his glass-work? What marvelous power made their dark reds, their intense blues and their snowy and steely pallors sparkle? I don't know; but those two figures attracted me invincibly. It would have been impossible for me to translate what they said to me; it penetrated into me by means of a magical language. It was like a filtration of voices from beyond the sea and radiance from beyond the sky. I gazed, I was fascinated, and dormant layers of memory stirred in the crepuscular depths of my soul.

Yes, for me, the virgin of the window and the knight of the terrible forest were fulgurant messengers from an unknown world, from a region that was distant, and yet more familiar than my surroundings. Such was my veneration for those two persons that I refrained from interrogating the chaplain on their subject. I was convinced that I knew them better than he did; his confused explanations would have troubled me in the secret worship so dear to my heart.

I recall exactly the day when a more intimate bond was established between me and the two immaterial beings painted on glass, whom I called in my silent monologues "the two angels of the chapel." Ought I to confide to you, unknown reader of this confession, these insensate things of my childhood, so dear to my memory that I tremble to write them? Perhaps I'm wrong and you're going to laugh at me, and yet it's from that mysterious moment that my better life emerged...

To enable you to comprehend my adventure, however, it's necessary for me to say something about the good chaplain who was charged with my education: I could do with him almost what I pleased, but I loved him dearly.

Oh, the good chaplain, with his well-nourished and clean-shaven face, and his broad features, whose creases had the heaviness of an old book of prayers with iron corners and Gothic characters, but which expanded in a benevolent smile as soon as he opened his mouth. He sat down facing me in a low room furnished with a little organ and a dresser filled with parchments; there he taught me sacred and profane history according to the Latin Bible and an old German chronicle that recounted the events of the human race from the fall of Adam to the Emperors of Germany.

Biblical and profane stories impassioned me, but they also caused me anxieties. The history of the human race seemed to me to be a lugubrious melee, like the engravings on wood from Nuremberg that ambulant merchants brought us, in which one saw naïve artisans, rich Pharisees, sinister rogues and executioners in turbans pressing around Christ in a frightful and compact crowd. On some days, my curiosity was amused by that pell-mell; on others a host of questions crowded my mind. I asked myself: "Why so much misfortune? Why so many wars? Why must we all suffer because of Adam's sin? Why have I been born in a century in which one hears talk of nothing but sacrilegious wars, when the Emperor's crown is sold at auction, and not in the time of the crusades?"

When I posed one of those questions to the excellent chaplain, I saw his face contract and a great furrow hollow out in his forehead. "God wanted it thus, my child," he stammered.

When I added: "But that is unjust, and I want to know why." he said to me, raising his large hand with a menacing index finger: "Beware of heresy! May the holy Church preserve you from the spirit of Satan!" Then his eyes expressed such terror that I had a desire to laugh, but I soon took pity on my master.

"Herr chaplain," I said, smiling, "I no longer want to know, and I will believe anything you wish, but this evening you'll give me, won't you, the book that contains the adventures of King Arthur?"

Immediately, the good priest's face lit up. "Konrad, Konrad," he said, "how much difficulty I have expelling your malign spirit! But I'll succeed in that; yes, I'll bind it with cords and precipitate it into the depths of Hell!"

As he concluded that sentence, in a resounding voice, the poor chaplain was reminiscent of Saint Michael transpiercing the dragon. I, who knew him, knew that I could obtain anything from him at such moments, and I added in a submissive voice: "Yes, my good father, you have defeated it forever; but you know, the book I need is the one that contains the story of Lancelot and Queen Guinevere."

"You shall have it," said the chaplain, "And now we'll sing a psalm and say a prayer..." And he placed his triumphant hands on the keyboard.

But that evening, in my somber bedroom, where Siegwart lay down beside me muttering stories of battle, the troubling questions returned to assail me. I rolled over in my blanket in order not to see the horrible crowd of the Nuremberg engraving, which surrounded me and jostled me: the murderers the executioners and the men in turbans threatening me with torture. Sometimes I woke up abruptly with an indescribable astonishment and a frightful fear of existence. It seemed to me then that a demonic power had hurled me out of nothingness, and I addressed questions to myself with a veritable bewilderment.

"Who am I? Why am I in the world? Why has the darkness give birth to me? How was I born from nothing?"

In the bright morning I slipped into the deserted chapel, I looked at the stained glass windows, and they consoled me a little. The knight of the terrible forest said: "Life is a battle!" and the virgin with the nimbus of streaming hair added: "Hope, my child; I can see the light!"

Among the books that the chaplain enabled me to read, I had a veritable passion for stories of the crusades. No other epoch of history attracted me as powerfully. The old oak dresser, our only library, contained a precious volume. It was a Latin chronicle brought back from a convent in Syria by one of my ancestors. It was written on parchment and difficult to read. I had the chaplain translate long chapters for me which he intoned with the emphatic voice of a church cantor. I listened to him, and my mind wandered in Palestine with the crusaders. I shall never forget the singular emotion I felt on the day when he read me the following passage:

The Christian knights were camped on the Syrian coast, near the mouth of the river Nasr-el-Ramyn, facing Saint-Jean-d'Acre, to which they had laid siege. Around them flourished the roses of Sharon, beloved by the daughters of Israel, and the great lilies of the fields, at which the Sons of God smiled, gazing at their virginal blooms. One morning, the crusaders saw five hundred ships arriving by sea, with all sails aloft, bearing the standards of the Cross. Those vessels were bringing new crusaders from Frisia, Denmark, France and Germany. A cry of joy rose up from the fleet and the Christian camp; the crusaders ran toward the shore to salute their brothers. But Saladin, the redoubtable sultan, the great enemy of Christ, taking advantage of that moment of confusion, threw his troops upon the posts that the Christians occupied on the sea shore, drove them back and entered the city. Then a great cry of indignation and rage ran through the camp of the crusaders. There were cries of "Saladin! Saladin, the enemy of God, the king of Babylon, the vanquisher of Jerusalem, has entered Saint-Jean-d'Acre!"

The interior vision that the story in question provoked in me had an almost supernatural precision. At the first words I felt that I was transported beneath a dazzling light. Before me the yellow sands of the Syrian beach snaked away as far as the eye could see, between a double band of sea and mountains staged in blue domes. I also saw rose-bushes like enormous bouquets blossoming in gardens planted with palm trees, and pale lilies of an unknown pride looking up amid the stones of hills.

Then, on the edge of a marshy plain, a fortified city launched like a peninsula into the sea designed its black walls and square towers. I could see the wooden towers of the besiegers distinctly. The coats of mail and helmets of latter were scintillating, and human clusters were tumbling from ladders. I also saw, on the ramparts, a swarm of multicolored coats and Saracen turbans. The name of Saint-Jean-d'Acre, heard for the first time, traversed me like a trumpet blast. It made me vibrate all the way to the marrow of my bones, and the enthusiasm of the crusaders lifted me up entirely, like a ship borne aloft by a wave. That of Saladin, on the other hand, touched me like the point of a dagger. I saw red and I had the sentiment of falling helplessly into a forest of scimitars and curved swords.

The sensation was so violent that I stood up and quit the chaplain instantly, alleging my lesson in arms with Siegwart. In reality, an irresistible desire drew me toward the chapel.

At the first glance cast toward the stained glass windows, they appeared to me to be brighter than usual. Was it the sun that was coloring them, or had a mysterious life entered into the windows? The virgin with the hair streaming like a nimbus around the face was resplendent in a fulguration of blood, gold and light, which sprang from her diaphanous and transfigured body. Was she trying to speak to me?

Immediately, I saw the tulip that she was holding catch fire, and I felt a profound commotion in my heart That torch—I had understood now—was her own heart. It was burning without being consumed, burning with an eternal love for the person she loved, and its red flame, its bloody flame, was showing him the route of splendors...

I looked at the knight. His attitude and expression had changed. He seemed now to be launching himself out of the ogive, his eyes ablaze, and his gaze darted into the gloom like a thin ray, toward the flamboyant heart of the martyr. I even asked myself, sometimes, whether he and I might not be one and the same person, and that thought gave me a frisson of pride.

Such was my life of dream, hidden in the utmost depths of myself, nothing of which was betrayed externally. It shone in the night of my soul like an intangible lamp in a closed sanctuary. But I had another, anxious and seething, as if released from outside. Hunting and excursions of horseback carried me into the woods. I departed early in the morning with Siegwart, my crossbow on my back and a quiver of arrows at my saddle-bow. As soon as we had crossed the ditch of the castle I became another person. The bright birch-trees quivered over the dark pond, blackbirds chirped in the hedges.

With what a palpitation I entered into the great arcade of beeches! Last year's dead leaves crackled under the hooves of my horse, but the new year's leaves, swollen by sap, babbled over our heads in melodious frissons. In the coolness of the profound wood, the rising morning sun sowed silvery splendors. The moving latticework of branches was dotted with a thousand holes of light. Oh, the first gust of the forest, which the odor of damp earth was mingle with the ligneous scent of the trees and the perfume of wild flowers! It intoxicated me, multiplied my being a hundredfold. There was a blossoming of all my senses in the breath of the forest.

I experienced an intense sensuality in living a thousand lives through my dilated eyes, my attentive ears and my excited sense of smell, and all my open pores. I absorbed the songs of the birds, the cries of beasts and the murmur of the leaves. I felt myself becoming, by turns, the vigorous oak, the babbling stream, the bounding roe-deer, the yapping dog, and the rapid falcon that I launched toward its aerial prey by removing its leather hood.

That initial intoxication was soon mingled with an impetuous desire for conquest and possession. The pursuit of a red deer or a capercaillie began, breathlessly, through the thickets. The gilded plumage of a bird or the tawny fur of a lynx fixed my desire. I discovered in myself, not without fear, the savage instincts to which hunting and war give birth, the thirst for blood and the pleasure of killing. But fits of black remorse and bitter sorrow traversed my intoxications, and I remember having wept for an entire week after having grievously wounded a hind that had not wanted to abandon her fawn.

Those mad chases through the woods only acted on the surface of my being, however. A profound disturbance soon upset them: that of woman. It did not come to me from one woman alone, but from the entire sex. At the age when the senses awake, from further away than I could see, women appeared to me simultaneously as the supreme seduction and the most redoubtable of enemies.

Sometimes, we went for long rides in the plain. In the month of May, near villages and hamlets, on Sundays, I saw peasants of both sexes coming out to dance. They went down on to lawns, the women in multicolored dresses, coiffed with their chapel hats, the young women crowned with verdure. At their noisy and vulgar gaiety I felt a mixture of disdain and desire. Their gestures and words shocked me, but in their insensate joy I divined that to be part of a couple is the only happiness.

One day, I came across a round dance around a linden tree, to the sound of a precipitate tune. The peasants perceived me at a distance. Immediately breaking the circle, the troop snaked into the meadow, the fiddler at the head. The saraband drew nearer in a spiral. I stopped surprised. They formed a circle around my horse, continuing to dance to the sound of the violin, with great leaps. Girls and boys invited me to join the dance, and, when I made no response, the peasant girls threw flowers at my face. Then they took hold of their dancing-partners again, and the couples returned, arm in arm to the linden. Cries of joy resounded, punctuated by kisses.

I resumed my route, humiliated, harassed and red with shame. I revolted against the vulgarity of the villeins. The savage cries had whipped my blood, however, and the kisses of the rustic couples burned my neck. I went back into the forest like a wounded animal. Passing over the drawbridge of the castle again, I thought myself accursed in my lordly solitude.

Another adventure finished enfevering me. I was coming back late through a narrow valley in the grassy depths of which a sinuous stream ran. Moonlight was sliding furtively between dark clouds. In places, pools of water glistened like silver basins. I perceived a mill half-hidden by clumps of alders. Light laughter was coming from it, in a splash of water. I pushed my horse through the dense shadow of the trees and stopped, fascinated.

Facing me on the opposite bank, a white form was outlined by the moonlight in the darkness of the boscage. The naked bather, having escaped from the bath, emerged from the long grass like a human flower with nacreous flesh, and combed her long hair, which was mingled with vegetation. Huge pale pink flowers raised their poisonous blooms amorously toward the woman, and the woman teased the flowers lasciviously with the black serpents of her hair. With a languorous gesture she bent down and intoxicated herself with their perfumes. Then, suddenly straightening up, she displayed the lustrous mass of her hair in the moonlight with a superb slowness and wove a tenebrous aureole, a diadem of somber voluptuousness.

Was it the miller's daughter who was taking her bath under the cover of the night and the alders? Was it the nixie of legends, a beautiful soulless body that acquires life by drinking the souls of men and drawing them into the depths of the water? She seemed to be undulating in the caresses of the nocturnal star, a jealous watcher. I gazed at her, avid and terrified; I devoured her with my eyes; my blood was hammering in my arteries.

Suddenly, my frightened horse whinnied and started. The bather uttered a scream and dived into the water. My horse carried me away. A moment later I stopped on the road, nailed to the spot by a burst of laughter. A woman's voice launched into the night the clear notes of a mocking refrain.

You who are returning from the crusades,
Ha ha! Why search for your people?
Ha ha! Your beauty is no longer here.
But under the lake, handsome comrade,
Under the green and transparent surface,
The arm of a girl
A glistening breast,
Awakens your heart! The Nixie is there!
Ha ha!

I departed at a gallop, spurred by a hundred demons. Woman, an elementary power, attracted me with an extreme violence; and I fled the temptress, fled at a sonorous gallop, with a frightful presentiment of my destiny. Returned to the thickets of the forest, blue-tinted by the moonlight, I tried to collect myself, but in vain. An unknown and fatal force had taken possession of me.

To soothe my swollen chest, I sent into the nocturnal silence of the woods a resounding fanfare, a savage halloo. Oh, that halloo! How many times I was to repeat it in the course of my life! Already, then, the willful child was calling, evoking unaware, from the depths of darkness, the daughter of Eve, the multiple Chimera, the eternal Deceiver, the Illusion made flesh. But, an insensate hunter, I did not know that I was my own prey, that in my hectic course I would redden with the blood of my heart the brambles of the path and the bark of the oaks.

The next day, when I went into the oratory, the knight of the stained glass had his most somber expression, and the terrible monsters of the forest covered me with their voracious eyes. The virgin martyr was so pale, so very pale that she seemed to be dying on her glass. I invoked her by turns as one invokes a mother, a sister or a fiancée. For all response I saw two tears trembling on the edges of her eyes. Like two limpid droplets they trickled down the window. Then I felt my own eyes also becoming moist, and I went out, weeping. What, then had happened to me?

In that epoch my father returned to Felseneck. He was a taciturn man with a hard heart and a sharp eye. One night, he was chatting in the great hall of the castle with one of his neighbors, a joyful and indefatigable drinker. A large oak log was ablaze in the large hearth of the hall of honor. In the heights of the colossal chimney a March tempest was howling and groaning like an army of demons. I had entered the obscure hall soundlessly, impelled by I know not what anguish. I remained hidden in a retreat not far from the fireplace. Neither of the two interlocutors had seen me. My father, sitting close to the fire, was poking it. The other was emptying his tankard repeatedly.

"You're wrong to have quit the Elector Palatine for the Emperor," said the cheerful companion. "You won't collect either fief or glory, and you'll lose the greater part of your fortune."

"It doesn't matter," said my father. "I don't like the Elector. Didn't he promise me the fief and castle of Staufen three years ago? He's given them to a guitar-plucker who doesn't even know how to hold a lance in a tourney, whom he's made into his cup-bearer."

"Stay here, then, and marry again."

"I won't take another wife. I was only married to Hilde for a year, but it wasn't happy. She was as transparent as the saint of the window in the oratory she had constructed and my approach made her shiver. Alive I loved her, and dead I hate her; I knew that she loved someone else. Women bring bad luck to Felseneck."

"Do you know that, listening to you, I sometimes wonder whether what people say about your family is true?

"What do they say?"

"That a malediction hangs over you."

"What malediction?"

"You know that in the time of the Emperor Barbarossa your family was divided into two branches, the Staufens and the Felsenecks, always rivals. The Staufens, who were the more bellicose, almost all perished in the Emperor's war with Henry the Lion.[1] Their last scion, Konrad von Staufen, was betrothed to Berthe of the Seven Winds,[2] the unique heir of the castle of that name; but Konrad left for the crusades and was killed it's said, in a battle outside Saint-Jean-d'Acre. His fiancée didn't want to believe that he was dead and waited for many years in her castle, after which she died of languor.

---

[1] Henry the Lion (c.1130-1195) was Duke of Bavaria from 1156-1180. He was the cousin of Emperor Fredrick Barbarossa (1122-1190) so his "war" with Henry was actually a family feud, soon settled, after which the later remained loyal.

[2] This title is given in the original as *Sept-Vents*, which would be *Sieben-Winde* in German, but it seemed simpler to use the English translation.

"By virtue of that death, the two families of Staufen and Seven Winds being extinct, their heritage passed to their cousins, the Felsenecks; but the father of the abandoned woman, in despair at the death of his daughter, pronounced against the heirs that profited from the disaster of his family a redoubtable malediction. He wished that all the Felsenecks would suffer and perish via their wives, as his daughter had suffered and perished by virtue of one of theirs. 'As for the last of the race,' he said, 'he will expiate for all the others.'"

"Yes, I know that that's what nurses and witches say about my family. Tales of Bohemians and wandering minstrels! I know that Castle of the Seven Winds, which one of my ancestors sold: a nest of foxes and owls, well worth the trouble of such a curse!"

"Why, then, has no one ever dared to rebuild the walls fallen into ruin? The certain thing is that the malediction has struck. You confess yourself that the Felsenecks have not been fortunate with their wives. Among your ancestors, one ran away with a Hungarian lord, another poisoned her husband, a third threw hers into an oubliette in order to live with her nephew. You married an angel of grace and beauty, but you lost her after two years of marriage without having been able to make her love you, and your only son bears the penalty of it, for you give the impression of detesting him. In truth, my dear, that resembles a curse, or at least a singular fatality."

"And all that happened to us because one of our ancestors died gloriously at Saint-Jean-d'Acre instead of marrying the daughter of an old graybeard? Strange justice, in truth!"

"Yes, but a mystery hangs over the fate of Konrad von Staufen. It's said that he didn't die outside Saint-Jean-d'Acre and that..."

"You're lying, wretch! Not one word more!" my father said, in a sudden fit of fury. He brandished the iron poker, red-hot from the fire, and was about to strike his companion in arms with it. The latter had risen to his feet, his tankard in his hand; he tottered and let himself fall, mouth open, into a high ancestral seat. Half-sobered, he was trembling like a leaf.

"It's fortunate that you're drunk!" said my father. Otherwise, I believe I'd have killed you. But don't permit yourself to talk about my ancestors and the secrets of my family again. If not, I might inflict on you the fate that one of my gallant ancestresses reserved for her husband, and you'd risk ending your days in a oubliette."

In order to conceal his fear, the cheerful companion uttered a loud burst of laughter. The howls of the storms resounded to it in the chimney, and the glimmers of the flame, reflected from old armor, animated momentarily the hollow images of those ancestors, of whom I sensed a sinister presence at that moment, diffused in the darkness.

I let silently, as I had come. Having returned to my room, I rolled myself up in a woolen blanket on my bed, my head feverish. The wind was raging in the towers and stairwells of the castle. Its cavernous voice whistled in ascending sales, to descend again with a dull roar and then climb yet again. In the same fashion, my thoughts rose and fell in my soul, in swirling spirals, rushing from ancient terrors to new desires only to plunge again into the most profound terrors. The bizarre conversation of my father and his companion blazed before me in letters of fire and obsessive images.

Why was that curse upon my family? Why, then, did I experience an inexplicable but irresistible sympathy for the man who was the cause of it, Konrad von Staufen, the crusader vanished at Saint-Jean-d'Acre? Why, also, the strange frisson that the mere name of the Castle of the Seven Winds had given me, suddenly evoked: the tomb of the mysterious abandoned woman?

The destiny of my family opened beneath my feet like a profound crypt into which I was obliged to descend in order to solve the enigma of my own. Engaged in the dark stairway, however, I appealed in vain to my dead mother, the dear mother I had never seen, and to the virgin of the window, to guide my tremulous steps with their gentle light. The more I delved into the problem, the darker it became around me.

Then, weary of my search, I uttered a cry of revolt. Invoking God and challenging destiny, I abandoned my soul to the wind that was raging outside, whipping the trees and assailing the walls as if to uproot the paternal castle. An unknown force lifted me up, a new thirst for action, amour and sacrifice.

"Well, yes," I said to the tempest, "tear my away from here, and carry me beyond the sea, to the shore of the crusaders!"

And I flew away. Mountains and plains passed beneath me, confused, and I thought I could hear the savage growling of waves colliding in the darkness of the abyss. I went to sleep with my nightmare, and all night long I traveled through the air...

Today, as I relive my life in my thought, I see myself as a poor bird carried away by the wind, which sometimes dozes off, its wings extended, in the torment.

At daybreak, an idea came to mind like a flash of lightning. Might I not find some details about the siege of Saint-Jean-d'Acre, and the enigmatic ancestor, in the old chronicle forming part of my family archives, from which the chaplain had read me passages? I ran to the dresser and took out the dusty manuscript.

It was impossible for me to understand a single word of that old grimoire with tangled characters. I was crumpling it with chagrin when my attention was attracted by a sheet of white papyrus stuck to the yellow parchment. It was covered in tiny Arabic writing in red ink, with abundant Oriental flourishes and volutes. On the other side of the sheet there were a few lines in Latin, in black ink, in an elevated and rigid script. At the first glance I shuddered. I had seen, inscribed in capital letters, the name KONRAD VON STAUFEN.

I was dazzled; the letters danced before my eyes. Finally, though, I was able to read:

The Grand-Master of the Order of the Temple has received from the Sultan of Egypt the enclosed letter relating to Konrad von Staufen, Knight of Christ, who disappeared at Saint-Jean-d'Acre in the year 1180 of the Christian Era. He has transmitted it to Otto von Felseneck, heir of the properties situated in Germany of the aforesaid Staufen, is order that he might make such use of it as he wishes.

Beneath those lines was the seal of the Order of the Temple. Beside it the Grand-Master had drawn with the pen the Felseneck arms: a griffin on a black field. His proud and angular handwriting had framed our blazon with two mottoes. He had written above: *Patefacta erunt dei arcane* (the Arcana of God are manifest); and below: *Ultimo veritas...*

At first I could not translate the second motto, but the meaning penetrated me abruptly, like a shock. An interior voice, the Voice of Silence, spoke within me and pronounced the redoubtable sentence: "To the last of your race, the truth…and that last will be you!"

That thought transpierced me like a ray of light. At the same time, it seemed to me that the malediction of the Lord of the Seven Winds fell with all its weight upon my innocent head. My seizure was such that I did not make the slightest start or utter a cry. Motionless, my throat taut, I was suffocating. I felt that I was under the hand of destiny.

I had collapsed on a chair, the book open on my knees.

Finally, I stood up again. "I have the secret," I said to myself. "Come what may, I want to know, and I shall."

Carefully, I detached the sheet of papyrus from the parchment and I put all my care into sewing it with my own hands into a velvet sachet, my mother's work. I knotted the sachet with a gold chain, which I passed around my neck, and I hid the precious object under my garment.

That sheet will no longer quit me, I thought.

An hour later, I traversed the courtyard of the castle in order to go to see Siegwart, who was teaching me to handle a lance. My father passed the hunting falcons in review, arranged on their perches. His curt voice gave orders and scolded the falconer, who stood before him trembling, his back curbed. For myself, the night and the dawn had transformed me. I felt matured by ten years and taller by a cubit. The secret of my ancestors was now sleeping on my breast; the velvet sachet contained it. And that black heart, the heart of mourning that I was wearing over my own living heart, beating youthfully, filled me with a strange pride.

And in the utmost depths, the soul of my mother seemed to penetrate me with its mildness and its melancholy and sustain me in my secret struggle against paternal oppression. I had stopped, and I considered my father with new eyes. He had just caressed a falcon after having given it a morsel of raw flesh.

His eyes encountered mine.

"What are you doing there?" he asked, brusquely. "And why are you looking at me like that?"

"I was thinking about my mother," I replied, with a candid boldness.

He started with astonishment, and his bitter gaze seemed to say: "How he resembles her!"

Then he resumed his dry tone: "Always in your dreams instead of at your weapons! Get ready; we're leaving for Nuremberg tomorrow. It's necessary for me to be there when the Emperor passes. In three months you'll enter the service of the Elector Palatine as a page. It's time to emerge from the nest and win your knight's spurs."

A flush of blood and joy rose to my brain at the idea of traveling and seeing the vast world.

At sunset, I went solemnly to say my adieux to the virgin of the stained-glass window. A ray of light illuminated her entirely. She smiled in her ecstasy, as if to say: "Go in peace, my child! The light that is upon me will be in your heart."

II. The Astrologer of Nuremberg

Nuremberg! The city of a hundred towers and thousands of gables, where the palaces are painted with red giants with chubby cheeks and winy flesh, where wrought iron fountains loom up in the middle of the market like cathedrals; Nuremberg, the queen of imperial cities! My heart beat faster on seeing it from a distance, but I thought I might choke when I entered that forest of stone with innumerable points, overflowing with soldiers, burgers, prelates and princes. I started thinking about the other forest, that of beeches, firs and oaks, where the red deer bounded and the birds sang, and I began to regret my wild manse, my falcon's nest on the mountain.

My father and I were lodged with an old, rich and devout aunt. I can still see the corniced window embrasure where I was posted to watch out for the Emperor's entrance. My aged relative, a lady with a red face and round eyes clad in a heavy dress of gilded brocade, was sitting beside me. The window overlooked the main square, which was swarming with heads. In the middle, under a splendid awning, stood the magistrates of the city, in red velvet bordered with ermine. A high platform covered with a carpet and surmounted by a throne was facing them. The Emperor arrived, surrounded by a picket of lansquenets, who parted the crowd with broad seeps of their halberds, vociferating: "Make way for the Emperor!"

He appeared on horseback in a black velvet costume, the sun of the Golden Fleece shining on his breast. His red-bearded face seemed harsh and impassive. Two pages were carrying the golden globe and scepter before him on velvet cushions. Twelve princes of Germany followed on horseback. A great tumult rose in the crowd while the Emperor descended from his horse, aided by the process, and climbed the platform.

When he was installed on the throne, the burgomeister climbed the steps and, placing one knee on the carpet, presented the keys if the city to the sovereign. Still impassive, the Emperor took them and stood up. Then, with his right hand, he extended to golden scepter toward the immense crowd and toward the city. An immense acclamation rose up from the square, the windows, the roofs and the chimney-stacks, swarming with human clusters.

I felt submerged by the tide of delirious acclamation, the waves of which rebounded around me. And yet, I remained chilled with horror. In the depths of my heart, something—I know not what—rebelled against that irresistible power, which imposed itself on the world. As soon as the first appearance of the sovereign in his imperial majesty, I had seen floating around him a sinister yellow aura. Thanks to a singularity of my sight or my nature I had always seen that livid yellow aura floating around coffins and catafalques containing a cadaver. While the crowd howled in an intoxication of servitude, I recoiled, fearfully, before that aura of death and decomposition around its idol. Thousands of hearts, vanquished by the golden scepter, were exultant with joy; mine alone cried: "I don't want that!"

By virtue of an even stranger repercussion, the real vision produced an imaginary vision within me. Suddenly, I ceased to hear the shouting in the square; the noise of fifes and drums ceased to strike my ears; I thought that I was transported to a vast lawn covered with multicolored tents, armed men in ancient costumes and horses covered with blankets with seigneurial blazons. A monk was preaching under an oak to the undulating crows. Brilliant knights were furrowing the plain as if in a tourney. The silhouette of Nuremberg was outlined on the horizon with its towers and steeples, dominated by its castle. Suddenly, an emperor and several kings on horseback emerged from a tent embroidered with a red cross. The sovereigns wore a similarly colored cross over glittering armor. All hearts were beating freely. Princes, knights and people were enveloped by a silvery glow that lifted them up on joyous waves, and the same cry that emerged from the crowd sprang up in my heat: "The cross! The cross! To the Holy Land!"

Everything had disappeared for me; I was dreaming while awake. Suddenly, I felt myself shaken. My aunt was looking at me with her round eyes and her face convulsed with anger.

"See," she said to her neighbors, "this wretched child who hasn't opened his mouth and doesn't want to salute the Emperor! See how he's frowning; that's the sign of the evil spirit. Just wait, little savage! I'll send for the canon to confess you!"

After my unexpected rapture, my aunt's face appeared to me so ugly, her voice so vulgar, and her soul so basely malevolent in her stupid devotion that I fled from the room and from the house into the street. Impelled by my interior demon, I frayed a path violently through the compact crowd, sliding like an eel between the lansquenets and the horses. The world, the crowd and life horrified me. I needed silence and meditation in order not to burst into sobs of rage. At hazard, I took refuge in a large church.

It was almost deserted. The profound nave shone like a finely-wrought reliquary with its slender pillars, its delicate ogives and its painted statues. Liturgical chants coming from the choir wandered under the vaults. The contrast of those celestial voices with the imperial masquerade did me good. I knelt down next to a marble font sustained by angels with unfurled wings and stammered a prayer whose meaning was: "My God, give me someone to love and show me the way."

At the same time I felt my immense solitude; tears began to well up. In order to stop them flowing, I raised my eyes instinctively toward the somber vault, but they escaped regardless and trickled silently over the dusty paving stones.

At that moment I perceived a tall, thin and curbed old man coming toward me. He was clad in a fur-edged mantle and a velvet beret. His elongated face with delicate features was furrowed by wrinkles, and had a waxen pallor. He must have been very old, but his expression was placid and majestic. He stopped and fixed his large eyes on me, which were shining like veiled lanterns.

We looked at one another momentarily. Eventually, in a soft and profound voice he said: "Praying with so much fervor at your age...that's very strange. Have you some worry, my child?"

I was ashamed of being fathomed in my most secret thoughts, and I replied, blushing: "No, none."

"But your soul is ill," he went on. "You can talk to me. I'm a physician of the soul."

No human gaze had ever penetrated like that one into the depths of my heart. An unknown confidence rose within me like a surge of vital warmth.

He went on: "Tell me why you're sad,"

"Noble lord," I replied, "my father is my entire family. He doesn't love me and I can't love him. He wants to present me to the Elector Palatine and engage me in his service. I'll obey, but I'll be unhappy. I'd like to serve and follow a lord I could admire, but I have no guide or master. Yes, I'm alone, always alone since my childhood."

"Alone...yes, alone!" said the old man, nodding his head and raising his pale hand, rendered almost transparent by a ray of sunlight falling from a high window. "They're alone, all those who are suffering and expiating: no one understands them, and they don't understand themselves. That's the ineluctable Law. I, too, march under the Law, but God has allowed me to understand the suffering of others, and now I'm no longer alone. For one who is able to read souls possesses countless brothers, and one who can cure them participates in the Light of the World... But you poor child, your eyes are anxious; child of desire, your ardent and fleeting soul is like a candle vacillating in the wind.

He was looking at me with a paternal tenderness. Strangely enough, I was moved by his words without understanding them. I listened to him avidly, sometimes delighted and sometimes fearful. I shivered under the syllables that fell from his lips as if beneath the voice of Providence, and each of his enigmatic words was engraved in letters of fire in the depths of my being awakened with a start. By virtue of an irresistible impulse I seized his fallen arm with one hand; with the other I clung convulsively at the fur of his mantle, crying: "Be my master, I beg you!"

He touched my shoulder, then took my head by the temples and looked at me even more intently. "You said *master*? You really said that?"

"You are my master, because I love you and I believe in you."

"Divine wisdom! Look at the Soul! Presence of God be blessed, I salute you in this child!" the old man went on; and he placed his hand on my head and stroked it gently. "You have said it my son; to believe is to love and to love is to know. It has been promised to me for a long time: 'A consolation will come to you, the solitary and the accursed, in your old age. A child will be found on your route who will call you *my master*. He will love you, and you will love him, but your joy will be as fleeting as a ray of light that shines in a church window. However, you will be to one another a smile of Heaven. He will announce your impending deliverance to you, and you will give him a cordial for the road of life and that of eternity.' God be praised! That consolation, that child, is you. I'm sure of it now."

"Oh," I cried, "in order to live with you I'll quit my father and my castle!"

"Poor child, they won't let you come to me," he said, sadly. "If you fled your home and I kept you in my house, they'd accuse me of having bewitched you, and they'd end up burning both of us. They're always accursed, those who prefer the eternal truth to human authority and power. Those who seek the hidden God are jeered. But listen; it's necessary that I see you one more time. I want to read your destiny; I want to know who put you in my path. Come to see me this evening, at nightfall, in Sebaldstrasse. Go as far as the little house on the corner near the round tower. On the sculpted wooden door you'll see the name *Rupertus*. Beneath it you'll read the words: *Magister artis et scientae. Doctor utriusque medicinae*. Lift the metal hammer and let it fall back. I'll open the door myself and take you into my sanctuary. Until this evening! We'll only need one supreme meeting. It's necessary that no one catches us together. Until this evening...until this evening!"

He enveloped me with a melancholy gaze shook my hand forcefully and drew away at a slow pace. Motionless. I watched him walk along the long nave. I felt happy, reassured, as if in a pleasant dream. For the first time, someone had spoken in the utmost depths of my soul, and the thing was so marvelous that I wondered whether the old man, gliding between the pillars, might not have emerged from one of the stained glass windows of the cathedral.

"Who is that man?" I asked a passing sacristan.

"Master Rupertus!" he said, with a grating accent of hatred and a scandalized expression. "An astrologer and a sorcerer. Beware of him!"

The sacristan threw holy water over me and went away, making a large sign of the cross. I remained astonished momentarily. Then I looked at the handsome marble angels who were sustaining the font with their wings. I seemed to see them smile. That smile said: "Don't worry; Rupertus is one of our family, but when we pass among humans, they cannot recognize us."

That evening, I succeeded in escaping my aunt's surveillance. The bells of Nuremberg were ringing the curfew; the darkening city was tightening its forest of towers and gables in a pink twilight when I slipped into the narrow and solitary Sebaldstrasse in order to knock on the master's low door.

He came to open it himself. I followed him up a spiral staircase and through several small low rooms into what he called his sanctuary. It was a high and vaulted circular room which occupied all the width of an old round tower adjacent to the house. It served him simultaneously as a library, a laboratory and an astrological chamber. A copper lamp of antique form, fixed to a bracket, was illuminating with its smoky wick the manuscripts and folios spread on a work table near the unique lattice window pierced in the thick wall.

Pell-mell in the chamber stood, as if animated by a magical life, several small iron stoves and two enormous cardboard globes sustained by wooden struts, one representing the Earth and the other the sky, with the signs of the zodiac. Along the walls, stacked on wooden shelves, were large books, the skeletons of animals, and bottles of every size. Above the shelves, around the perimeter of the rotunda, seven globes of various colors represented the seven planets. Each globe supported a statuette in painted wax. Each figure held its sign in its hand: sun, sword, mirror, or scythe, sickle, lightning-flash or caduceus; the entire ensemble watched over that refuge like tutelary divinities. The spider-webs that hung down from the obscure vault formed vague constellations there.

"Behold my universe," said Rupertus, sitting down slowly in a large armchair with a leather back. "I have no other domains than these dusty spheres; no other friends than these books; no other protectors than these mute genii; no other sky than this vault. Would you like to live with me?"

"Oh, yes, I'd like that!" I exclaimed. "But all this is strange. I've never seen anything like it. About what do all those books speak? What do those bizarre signs mean, and those pale figures looking at us from above? I don't know, and yet I feel happy here, with you, as if I had always lived here. It seems far from what I hate and what oppresses me, and close to everything I love...and which I've never seen. Oh, my master, my friend, tell me why I'm happy here, as if I were at home."

"It's because, you see, my child, this room is the image of the world; it smiles at you because the human fatherland is not a corner of the earth but the entire universe."

"Is that possible? Oh, explain it to me, I beg you."

"Gladly. But come closer and give me your hand. That's good; now listen. The sky, with its stars, is the image of God. The earth obeys its ineluctable laws, it submits to the influence of the planets. But man, that other image of God, is also a universe. He has his atmosphere, his planets and his sky. He obeys the signs under which he is born and which are imprinted in the organs of his body. He can struggle against them, but cannot avoid them. When the soul, the daughter of Heaven and the word of God, is incarnate down here, it is enclosed in a narrow circle in which it rotates fatally. Only death can break it. Then it recovers its liberty, by returning to the Invisible, and resumes possession of the infinite universe. That is why, my son, your soul quivers with joy before the sacred signs of the secret forces that are the light of Nature and the radiance of the eternal Word. Before them, it senses its future liberty and salutes its fatherland."

At that moment, a spider let itself fall from the height of the vault and remained suspended by its thread above the astrologer's table. It seemed to be charmed by a crystal ball as large as an apple mounted on a little marble plinth and placed amid the folio volumes. The light of the lamp made the transparent globe shine. The spider was visibly fascinated by the iridescence of the shiny little sphere, through which it thought it could see flies passing.

Rupertus turned the parchment of a large book, and the spider, frightened, returned to the vault.

"You see," the old man continued, "it wanted to move out of its fatal circle, but it couldn't escape from it. Dazzled momentarily by the crystal ball, it is climbing back anxiously to its darkness and returning to the center of the web that it has woven itself... There is the image of the man who wants to cast a glance beyond his earth."

"But afterwards, after death, where do we go" I asked, anxiously.

"Look at the stars and then look into yourself; then reply. The soul that listens finds itself at the center of life. Our Lord said: 'In my father's house there are many mansions,' and the Holy Spirit said to the Elect: 'There are many lives after this life.' But a truce on speech; if you and I have encountered one another, it is not at the hazard of elements colliding in chaos, it is by the will of God, in order that our souls can speak to one another and say something eternal. Come closer, in order that I can look into the depths of your eyes."

I moved closer to him. Gently, he passed his aged hands through the thick curls of my hair, and then placed them on my shoulders.

I observed him confidently. I would have liked to spread out before him my most secret life in a single gaze, like a flower opening and yielding all its perfume.

He continued: "I could search for your destiny in this book"—he pointed to a large volume bearing the title *Astronomia magna*—"but I would need to know the day of your birth and draw up your horoscope.[3] Your

---

[3] The title cited is best-known as that of a book attributed to Paracelsus (1493-1541), but if that were the intended reference

destiny is not written on your naïve brow, in that anxious mouth and those eyes that are already burning with passions of which you're unaware. To desire recklessly, to suffer incessantly and without knowing why, to roll a rock like Sisyphus, to hunt the chimera, to pant after the impossible and fall back into the accursed rut...that is your destiny. What, then is the terrible malediction that weighs upon you?"

At the word *malediction* I started, and Rupertus exclaimed: "What's the matter?"

Until that moment the strangeness of the place had extracted me from my past. Transported by the master's words, I had had the sentiment of floating with him in infinite space, outside time, under the blinding or distant light of marvelous stars. But the fateful word returned me to the sentiment of reality. I remembered the secret of my family that I carried over my breast and I had the clear perception that the time had come to know the enigma.

I took the velvet sachet from my garment and tore the stitches apart. I seized the sheet of papyrus and I held it out to the master.

"Can you read that?" I said, trembling with curiosity.

He brought the lamp closer and leaned over the yellow paper.

"It's Arabic," he said. "I learned that language in Syria, where I was the physician of a Muslim prince. Where did you get this document?"

"I removed it from an old chronicle found in my father's castle. I know that the parchment relates to

---

it would be anachronistic, as the story is set in the mid-fifteenth century.

Konrad von Staufen, who died four hundred years ago at the siege of Saint-Jean-d'Acre. Konrad was the last of the Staufens, a collateral branch of the Felsenecks. I'm the last descendant of the two families, over which it's said that a curse has weighed since the crusader's death.

"Marvelous," said the astrologer; "you're well-informed. The Latin inscription in black ink is by the Grand-Master of the Templars. It affirms that this papyrus comes from the Sultan of Egypt, whose seal is here. In delivering this document to your ancestor the Grand-Master has refused to translate it. He adds that the mystery will be revealed to the last of his race. Have you understood?"

"Yes."

"Well, Konrad de Felseneck, would you like to hear the translation of this letter?"

"Yes, I beg you."

"Are you not afraid of the epigraph: *Ultimo veritas*...to the last, the truth? It's permitted to few men to know the truth in this world, for few men can support it. The veil of ignorance that envelops us is a wisdom of God and a clemency of nature."

"Master Rupertus," I cried, "I want the truth, for I'm not afraid of anything."

"That's good. Listen, then; I'm translating:

"In the year of the prophet 557, during the siege of Saint-Jean-d'Acre, the enemies of God dared to penetrate into the camp of the lions of Islam. The first assailants fell under the iron of the Muslims as the evil will fall on the last day of judgment; the others fled. Only one remained in order to recover his master's banner. After a desperate combat he was taken prisoner and taken before Saladin. The sultan, admiring his courage, offered him his life and the title of Emir on condition that he became a Muslim.

"'My name is Konrad von Staufen,' said the Christian knight. 'My fiancée is waiting for me in my native land. Kill me and you will know how one dies for the faith of Christ.'

"Saladin smiled. At a sign of his hand, a curtain opened and his daughter appeared, slender and proud, sparkling with precious stones and beauty. In her hand she held a golden cup containing an exquisite beverage.

"'Know this,' said the sultan; 'all those who have perceived Saladin's daughter without a veil have been put to death, but to you she brings life. Love her and you will be my son. Choose between the executioner's blade that summons you to the Christian Heaven and my daughter's cup, which summons you to the paradise of Mohammed.'

"The Christian knight made a movement to tip over the cup that Zeynab was holding out to him, but he encountered her eyes and they looked at one another. A supreme challenge emerged from the knight's eyes; a moist flame flowed from the ardent and tranquil eyes of the royal daughter. Finally, the knight trembled, took the cup, emptied it, and fell, struck down by amour, at the feet of his queen.

"In order to attach him more fully, Saladin circulated the rumor of the death of Konrad among the Christians. He had died for them and lived for Islam, by the will of Allah."

On the reading of that story, one thing surged forth vividly in my mind, dominating all my thoughts. That was the radiant image of the Muslim princess, a flower of flesh with dark eyes, enveloped in the blue-tinted night of her hair. I respired the voluptuous perfume of those tresses and the white breast emerging from a corolla of gems. I vibrated under the gaze, I drank the cup.

Suddenly, a gust of fire invaded my body, virgin of the pangs of desire; I felt the temptation of the blood in my temples; I thought that my arteries were about to burst and I cried out, almost madly:

"Oh, those eyes...! That woman...! Fortunate Konrad von Staufen, I would give my life for a hour of yours! That woman, Rupertus...I want her!"

And I thought I saw the beautiful Saracen floating in the penumbra.

As I spoke I had clung with a sort of frenzy to the old man's arm, as if to make him share my vision and my desire. But he shook me rudely and considered me with a severe expression that I had not yet seen in him.

"Come on!" he said. "Konrad von Felseneck, have you no shame or remorse before your ancestor's action? What! To betray the faith of Christ, the honor of a knight and the august symbol of the cross for a daughter of the harem! The fiancée did not betray hers. She languished in her castle, languished for many years, always waiting...and then she died."

"That's true," I stammered, astonished, lowering my head. "I forgot...hence, no doubt, the malediction...which weighs upon us all...and upon me! So, Konrad von Staufen never saw his fiancée again?"

"No, never."

"And they will never be able to see one another again?"

"Are you dreaming, my son? How would they be able to see one another, since they have been dead for four hundred years? He sleeps in the Muslim lands, she in her crypt in Germany. What wind could bring their dust together?"

"Didn't you say just now that there is another life"

"There is one; but there too, barriers loom up, and the soul bears its limits within itself. For the traitor who fails the Beloved, the treason becomes a black veil that is interposed forever between his soul and that of his victim, unless..."

"Unless?"

"Unless he reenters into the flesh and expiates. Do you understand what an expiation is, which lasts a life-time?"

At the word *expiation*, a frisson fell upon me; I felt it stream from head to foot like an ice-bath. And, no less vividly than the Muslim princess, the image of a sad abandoned woman surged forth phantasmally to my interior vision. And as if I had committed the crime myself, I murmured:

"Expiate...! Yes, expiate...! And console the Abandoned...!

Master Rupertus had risen to his feet. For a moment, his gaze hovered over me, flamboyant and fixed, like the eye of an eagle. He was observing me like a strange phenomenon. I no longer dared to look at him, and I remained plunged momentarily in a dolorous mystery. When I looked at him again his eyes passed from severity to fear, and from fear to compassion; and from the depths of their vast light, where I sought a refuge, a new tenderness inundated me.

His faint voice said: "Poor child!"

Then, talking to himself, he whispered words, the meaning of which I could not comprehend. But which remained with me, like all those fallen from his mouth.

"Strange," he said, "very strange. The force of images has caused the ineffaceable imprints... He remembers...and from the abysms of consciousness the ancient soul is rising again. Is that him...? But let's try to read his magnetic atmosphere."

And abruptly, Rupertus said: "Look at that crystal ball and don't move!"

The old man sat down in his armchair and began to examine the blue-tinted ball, which shone like a star in the midst of the folio volumes on the table, under the little lamp. I went into a kind of reverie, in which floating images passed before my eyes. as when one falls asleep.

It seemed to me that I saw the ball grow and become a vast vitreous sphere. I found myself at its center. The sphere reached the obscure vault and made it disappear as it swelled. At the circumference, in a gray penumbra, tangled vague serpentine forms moved, as if in water. That movement amused my momentarily, and then I experienced a kind of malaise. I ceased gazing at the crystal and returned my eye to master Rupertus. Leaning against the back of his armchair, he had closed his eyes; one might have thought him a statue in a cathedral or a saint half-asleep while praying.

He started saying enigmatic things again in a barely perceptible voice.

"Venus envelops him...Venus dominates him...he's captive in the inferior sphere... The sirens and the sphinxes of the elements...efflorescences of the interlaced flesh...are weaving around him an impenetrable vault..."

I heard him sigh profoundly. After a momentary pause he resumed:

"Very far away, very high, I see a soul of light floating...her features are hidden...she's wearing a long veil...a bridal veil...the violet star is scintillating on her forehead...the dying star...of love in mourning..."

Rupertus sat up straight in his armchair, his eyes still closed. His features were strained; he appeared to be making a violent effort. Eventually, he continued:

"Ah! She would like to descend and speak to him...but he cannot see her...oh, the veils are thick, the veils are heavy... She makes a gesture to part them...she cannot...too much darkness around him...but what is she holding in her hand? A rose? No...a red heart...her own heart! It is emitting a great flame! But the soul is rising again, and disappears... A ray from her flamboyant heart has fallen as far as him...."

At that last phrase I felt a burning sensation in my heart and a mild warmth on my forehead. I started and seized Rupertus by the wrist.

"Oh!" I cried. "The virgin with the flamboyant heart! The one I invoked in my mother's chapel...about whom I dreamed so much...you've seen her? She exists, then, elsewhere than in her stained glass? Oh, show her to me, take me to her...! And the knight in the terrible forest...it's me, then! Oh, the crusade, the crusade! Show me the road to the crusade and the good combat... To fight for her, for the Invisible, for her flamboyant heart...out there, far away, beyond the sea, in the Orient! I've often felt her near me... Oh, Master Rupertus, if I could see her once, only once...and then throw myself into the great battle!"

Master Rupertus had opened his eyes upon me again, limpid and as if bathed in a living ether. The profound harmony of his soul had effaced all his wrinkles momentarily and transfigured his face. He enveloped me with a complaisant gaze, put his hand on my shoulder again and held me embraced.

"Yes, my son," he said, "I like you thus. Your dormant soul is awakening. It's the invincible God who is speaking in you now. Yes, you shall see the Virgin with the flamboyant heart; you shall see her on the day of the combat...perhaps only on the day of the ship-wreck...

"Yes, every man is born for his crusade, but how few know it! The road is long to the eve of arms, longer still to the field of battle. You know full well, Konrad von Felseneck that a heavy destiny weighs upon you: the malediction of your race. It's necessary to set it aside before finding your crusade. Do you remember a solitary castle buried under brambles and under its own ruins? Its name is the Castle of the Seven Winds. Go there alone, thinking about your ancestor's crime, and there, in the brambles, among the stones where the Abandoned sleeps, pray for the soul of Konrad von Staufen. That will be your first step on the road of expiation."

At the name of the Castle of the Seven Winds the excruciating dolor of the Abandoned struck me for a second time. A new, more terrible frisson shook me entirely. The idea of going to the sad keep appeared insupportable to me. Turning my head away I said: "No, not that, Master Rupertus! The Castle of the Seven Winds frightens me...I'll never go there!"

Master Rupertus shook his head gravely. A smile of almost maternal indulgence stretched his features. "Didn't you say just now that you weren't afraid of anything? You see, my child, that everyone is afraid of something."

He continued, in a more solemn tone: "I've read your body; I've read your astral aura; I've read your immortal soul. I've assembled the signs and now I can see your destiny. But what I've seen I can't tell you; and by saying it, in any case, I would only hinder your effort. You must discover it for yourself.

"Poor child, you are going to flee over the somber ocean, chased by the tempestuous wind. A pale ray from on high will follow you...may you never lose it! Try to grasp it, and when the Angel who wears the bridal crown appears to you, drink her light. If you perceive the Angel, the Voice of Silence will speak to you; and if the voice speaks to you, you will hear the warrior fanfare. Then, gather your courage and follow it, to life or to death. But beware of the Sphinx, which has the face and breasts of a woman and the claws of a tiger...

I drank his words as one listens to a strange and distant music, as one gazes at a starry sky in which worlds and marvels of harmony float. And again, I experienced an almost celestial rapture. My heart unfurled its petals like a rosebud in spring, and my soul vibrated with all its strings, like an Aeolian harp in the autumn wind.

A bell in the city chimed heavily. I uttered an exclamation.

"Ten o'clock! All the houses are about to close, and if I don't go back, how will my father welcome me tomorrow? When he's irritated, his eyes resemble the oubliettes underneath the keep; one doesn't know what's lying in wait for you in the depths. Oh, Master Rupertus, what if I were not to go back, if I quit everything to stay with you?"

"Thank you," said Rupertus, whose eye glinted through a tear. "I can see that you love me, as I love you; it's the promised cordial. Yes, I would have liked to detach your luminous soul from your tenebrous body, as a carver of precious stones detaches the diamond from its matrix, but Destiny does not want that. It always separates related souls down here; God alone can reunite them. Listen! You're going to return to your father's house; it's necessary that your life follows his law. For myself, I shall soon quit this petty universe for the other. But I want to leave you a memory and give you a viaticum."

He went to fetch an iron casket in which rare jewels were heaped pell-mell: crystals, rubies, chrysoliths, sapphires and diamonds. The old man plunged his thin pale fingers into them, as if he experienced a secret voluptuousness in delving into his treasure and caressing the sparkling gems.

"You don't know the power of precious stones," he said. "They're the eyes of inanimate matter, the stars that the earth elaborates through the centuries in its profound night. They attract or repel beings, gazes, fluids and thoughts."

He chose from the mass a silver ring in the bezel of which a superb amethyst shone.

"Look at this stone," he said; "It's the star of love that shines in absence and in mourning. I give it to you as a talisman. We will not see one another again. But remember when you look at it that, even dead, your master is watching over you. It will guide you toward the one who ought to deliver you. In the deepest distress, speak to it; it will respond to you. But don't reveal to anyone the treasure of your heart; don't surrender the secret of your soul; it would be profaned.

A further chime from a nearby church made me shudder. Master Rupertus planted a long kiss on my forehead.

"Let's go," he said. "It's necessary for us to separate. All roads lead to the final goal. Thought, like light, pierces space. Those who seek, find; those who love one another, never quit one another. God acts through the soul, and the rest is mystery. All wisdom consists of putting a little eternity into that fleeting life."

He had risen to his feet, picked up his lamp and seized my hand. I cast one last glance of infinite regret over the books, the globes and the statues of that marvelous refuge in which the world had changed its aspect for me without me knowing how or why.

We went downstairs. He turned a large key in the lock and the little door to the street opened. I was mute with emotion. I covered the thin and bony hand of the old man with kisses. He placed that hand on my head and murmured: "God protect you!"

At the sign of his finger I moved away, in the radiance that his little lamp projected toward the black street.

"Keep the ring carefully, and keep it hidden until the day of enlightenment. Then, you can wear it."

Those were his final words. At the corner of the street I turned round. Master Rupertus was still standing motionless on the threshold, his arm extended and his lamp in his hand.

"Adieu!" I shouted.

And I fled into the darkness, stifling a sob.

When I emerged into the square, the city, bristling with steeples, was outlined like another Black Forest against the somber luminosity of the sky. The moonless night was splendid. Innumerable constellations were palpitating in its abysms. That sky, in which the astrologer had enabled me to glimpse the gulfs of the Invisible, appeared to me to be vaster and emptier in its clear and cold gaze. The veil of brute matter, torn momentarily, had closed again abruptly.

I stopped, struck with fear by the silence if the universe and my profound solitude. And yet, I felt that something ineffable had penetrated me, and that I was no longer alone, as before.

III. The Dream in the Ruin

When I was far from Nuremberg, the image of Rupertus retreated gradually into an inaccessible region. The effervescence of youth and the smoke of passion veiled it; but nothing could efface it. Every time that my profound soul vibrated, it was bound to reappear, lucid and imperative. It seemed to me then that my true consciousness was reawakened with it.

Without the ring that I carried on my person I would have ended up believing that I had been dreaming, but when I was alone I took the amethyst out of the velvet sachet and its melancholy reflection threw me into long dreams. What was the mystical betrothal that Rupertus had promised to me? Was I to celebrate it with a supernatural being or a living person? I did not know anything and I scarcely believed it, having never truly believed in anything except things seen by the eyes and touched by the hand. But when I looked at the stone of the ring, a sadness mingled with hope slid into my heart.

I almost lost my treasure, however, in the early days of my return to Felseneck. "Keep it hidden until the day of enlightenment," Rupertus had said to me, but an infantile pride caused me to forget that recommendation and caused my first repentance.

One bright morning, I put the ring on my finger, glad to make its stone glisten in the sunlight. Gaily, I showed it to the chaplain.

"Where did you get that jewel?" said the excellent man, anxiously.

"From Master Rupertus, an astrologer in Nuremberg. It's a talisman that brings good luck. He gave it to me himself."

The chaplain's eyes rounded with terror. His face took on a liturgical aspect. I savored his fear.

"Wretched child," he murmured. "You've fallen into the hands of the evil spirit. Satan will take possession of you. If you don't get rid of that ring, you're doomed forever. Give it to me."

"Never!" I cried, wildly, with such energy that the chaplain was afraid, as if I were possessed by the Devil, and he went away raising his arms above his head.

An hour later I was dreaming in the embrasure of a window, my eyes lost in the immense plain of the Rhine, when I felt an iron hand fall upon my shoulder. I turned around and I saw, tremulously, my father gazing at me with his evil eye. I understood immediately that the chaplain had betrayed me, in the excess of his supernatural dread. My father was in one of his fits of cold anger, which presaged dry thunderbolts.

"What are you doing here?" he said. "Magic, no doubt! Where did that ring come from? Don't try to lie, I know everything. So it's old Rupertus that you went to see in Nuremberg. He'll have taught you some trick of sorcery. But beware! Remember that spell-casters are struck by their own evil spells. You're going to give your ring to the chaplain immediately, who will throw it in the river. Woe betide you if I see it on your hand again!"

My father's orders did not suffer any reply; in him the punishment always surpassed the threat. I went out, lowering my head. I understood now the master's words: "Don't show the treasure of your heart to anyone; don't surrender the secret of your soul; it would be profaned."

But what should I do? Was I going to give the ring to the chaplain? Was I going to permit the superstitious imbecile to rob me of the sacred memory of Rupertus forever? Would it not be a treason toward my own soul to deliver to the enemy the pledge of the beloved master, and to abandon forever the saintly unknown that floated over my life?

No, I could not. After such cowardice, it would no longer be permissible for me to believe in myself. I resolved to hide my treasure far from the castle, in a safe place unknown to anyone.

Two leagues from Felseneck there is a profound and dense forest dominated by two sheer peaks, one of which is known as the Angel's Rock and the other the Devil's Rock. In a clearing of that forest stands an ancient tree named the Fay's Beech. It is said that, at that place, a white fay emerging from the tree once appeared to a local lord, a fervent hunter who was pursuing a hind. The fay had placed her hand on the forehead of the tracked animal; the dazzled hunter had fallen to his knees before the glare of that body as brilliant as snow. She disappeared almost immediately from his blinded eyes, but the plaintive soul of the lord had had such a great desire and amorous chagrin, people said, that he ceased hunting from that day on and became a monk.

The Fay's Beech seemed to me to be a favorable place to hide the precious ring; no one dared to touch the haunted tree. I put the ring into a silver casket locked with a key and then escaped from the castle without being seen by anyone.

I was streaming with sweat when I reached the five times centenarian beech. Twice the height of a man, the king of the forest had a wound, a great gaping hole in its bark. I succeeded n climbing it and deposited my treasure therein. I blocked the opening with a large stone, which I drove with heavy blows into the wound in the tree. And I thought: *As soon as I'm free I'll recover my ring.*

I drew away under the high forest that descends the gentle slope, and the dry leaves twisted under my feet with sinister cracklings. Here, the woods covered the mountain for leagues and leagues, and their interminable murmur muffled the sound of footfalls and the sadness of thoughts. One could believe that one was in an endless basilica with green vaults and grey columns, which, on one side, plunged into valleys, and on the other, reached the summits. One marches on and on through the high forest, and the feet trample the dead leaves, and the frameworks of giant beeches support with their bare trunks the verdant vault where the sun laughs and the birds twitter. Thus humans, on their obscure route, march incessantly in the shadow of death while, above their heads, the dream of eternal life sings.

And that day, I turned round more than once on the descent. I tried to see again the Fay's Beech in the twilight of the wood, but in vain, for it had disappeared long before behind the innumerable swarm of gray trunks, huddled in clusters. Then my heart contracted; it seemed to me that I had lost my only friend. Had I not buried in that terrible forest the jewel of my life, the star of my destiny?

I told the good chaplain that I had thrown the ring into a torrent, and he declared himself satisfied.

They arrived, the troubled years of my life. I had become, successively, a page, a squire and a knight at the dissolute court of the Elector. I found there the shameful decadence of chivalry. Oh, how far away they were, the stories of the crusades and the poems of the troubadours, when the ladies were chaste, or at least faithful to the unique lover, the heroes pure, and the cavaliers loyal! Gambling, drunkenness, rapacity, servile obsequiousness toward the powerful and cowardly cruelty toward the weak, venality in all charges; a pompous and grotesque elegance in fêtes and ceremonies; villainy and vulgarity in all mores: such was the reality of human society that appeared to me.

It seemed to me, at first, that I had entered a brigands' cavern and a place of debauchery. I felt nothing but horror and disgust. As I lived there, however, scorn turned to indifference and indifference into habitude. And from day to day, gradually, the poison that I breathed in the air infiltrated me. The depths of my being were not corroded; there were intangible arcana in my soul that the world did not suspect and which it could not reach. The life of the body, however, becoming stronger, silenced the noble hopes of the adolescent, and threatened to subjugate the entire soul. My savagery made me ashamed of my companions at first, but, while conserving my naïve pride, I gradually made the apprenticeship of life. I became rude and cynical externally, and then a gambler and a libertine.

My father having perished in a tourney, I found myself the possessor of all his property, the sole heir of the name of Felseneck. Hazard informed me, in that epoch, of the death of the astrologer Rupertus, of whom I had had no more news since our memorable interview in Nuremberg. At that disappearance of the only man that I had veritably loved and venerated, I was seized by a sharp regret and a poignant anguish. My father's tyranny had ceased to crush me; I was as free as a bird in the air; but at the same time, the only light that had ever illuminated my route and penetrated the depths of my soul was extinguished. I was condemned to isolation, and the more I mingled with society, the more abandoned I felt.

I was then twenty-three years old. Soon, the intoxication of the senses took possession of me, with the vertigo of liberty. The reckless desire for Woman, which had bitten me for the first time before the nocturnal bather at the mill, invaded me entirely; it had submerged the divine dream. While still a page, the women of the court, coquettish and futile, had caught me in the net; those first experiments had filled me with sadness and disgust, to such a extent that when the intoxication had passed, I had found the female heart empty and vain. But a savage and blind instinct impelled me to recommence the adventure incessantly.

Where did it come from, that ardent thirst, that bitter curiosity to explore the female sex in its undulating multiplicity? Before every woman who tempted my desire I rediscovered, alive in my flesh, the torturing dart that the nixie of the mill with the snowy body and the mocking voice had launched at me. I shivered then before an irresistible force, in which all the powers of nature and the mysteries of sex seemed to be concentrated. Afterwards, there was a mad hope of being subjugated by that woman, of being absorbed into her in possessing her. I emerged from the arms of each mistress with the sentiment of something indomitable and irreducible that she had not been able to attain and of which she had no suspicion.

I emerged debased in my own eyes, as if I had profaned a treasure before unworthy eyes. Then came hours of lassitude, in which the virgin soul awoke within my soiled body, red with shame. The dream of my pure adolescence surged forth before me: the saint of the window...and the sanctuary of Rupertus.

Oh, in those hours, how I cursed the brutal desire to possess and be possessed by the flesh, the cruel conqueror or vanquished coward. How I languished in an entirely different desire, to love and to adore, and to give myself freely and unreservedly to something superior! Oh, to throb with divine amour for a divine heart! But where was that something to be found? Where did that heart respire?

No, the Angel promised by Rupertus had not come to extract me from the elementary world. The fanfare that was to announce my crusade was not vibrating in my ears; and I was dispersed far from the light, in the darkness of death.

Seized by a somber despair, I withdrew to my natal castle, to Felseneck, and started hunting furiously. Driven by an interior demon, I found no repose within those walls. Scarcely had I gone to bed than fever took hold of me. Insomnia and nightmare divided my nights between then. At sunrise, a frightful anxiety, an inexpressible and irrational anguish threw me out of bed. I felt more tranquil on horseback and in the woods. The maternal forest cradled me with its shadow and it light, its chirping and its animal cries, its murmurs and its tempests. I no longer had any joy in killing game; I allowed the roe deer to bound away through the grassy clearings and the capercaillies to fly away noisily beneath the thickets of fir-trees steaming with resin, without even fitting my arrow to my crossbow.

Sadly, I saw them disappear and I said to them, in my foolish pity: "Fly, bound and live! When, then, will the arrow turn against the murderer? When will the prey kill the hunter?" And then I went away, besieged by hateful phantoms: nixies, sirens and ghouls. I pursued through their menacing melee an ungraspable dream, which had the pallor of a dead hope. Like a criminal, I was afraid of human faces, and when I perceived my shadow extended over the moving edge of the woods or the red sand of the path, I shivered with horror.

It was toward the decline of a hot and heavy summer's day. A storm had rumbled, lightning had flashed. Under the streaming rain, I had pursued a red deer all the way to the hollow of a tenebrous wooded gorge. Having lost the trail, I had fled over hills and vales; I had gone astray, far from the dogs and the beaters, in an unknown region.

Dusk had fallen, calm and gilded. The shivering trees shook bright droplets over my head. The brown tresses of the forests faded away into the night; in the gaps between the clouds, a gulf of wan greenish-blue opened. My horse, fatigued, was walking slowly and neighing at the opening of the sky, along a mossy path bordered by black firs.

Oh, how tired the poor animal was, and how weary I was, too! It stumbled as it traversed a ravine, and we found ourselves in the profound ditch of an old ruined castle. In front of me, at the foot of the great wall, I saw a rounded arch closed by a worm-eaten door. It was the entrance to the court of honor.

At the summit of the portal, two stone griffins sustained a mutilated escutcheon invaded by brushwood. A thick mantle of ivy covered the wall and allowed its long tresses of green leaves to fall back. Higher up, the façade loomed, with Gothic windows all closed. Behind, a perforated keep was outlined against the sky.

I dismounted, for I was exhausted. A penetrating charm retained me captive in the place.

Where was I, then? I had never seen that forest and that castle before. And yet, the old ditch, the dilapidated portal and the armories corroded by the vegetation emitted a familial smile, the peace of a abandoned cradle, dormant under a veil of forgetfulness, inviting the great final slumber.

I spotted a collapsed section of the enclosing wall. Ferns had made a natural bed there under a baldaquin of clematis, eglantines and honeysuckle. After having emptied the wine from my gourd I let myself fall into the niche.

The bitterness of my soul mingled strangely with the wild scents of the ditch. I heard a dog barking and a bell ringing in the distance, and the pink of the twilight died in the crowns of the beeches. The walls and the foliage were confounded in obscure masses; gray night fell.

I closed my eyes.

When I opened them again it was pitch dark, but the entrance door facing me was open, and vaguely illuminated by a light that seemed to be coming from above. Without reflecting, I went up the broad steps of a winding staircase. The dubious light fled before me, illuminating the disjointed steps where my feet were placed.

After a long ascent, I went into a high vaulted hall with mysterious depths. An oak log was blazing in the hearth, casting its gleams into the penumbra.

In the embrasure of a window, a woman in a violet velvet robe edged with black was sitting at a table, her head bent over a tapestry that was lost in long volutes in the gloom of the hall. Behind her, a Gothic stained-glass window represented an aged knight with a white beard in gleaming steel armor; the bright light of the window enveloped the embroiderer with an intense reflection. Placid and grave, she seemed to be waiting for someone while working. Her ivory needle progressed with a regular movement. Without knowing how, I found myself sitting opposite her; the table separated us.

She raised her transparent face toward me then. A blue headband circled her forehead with a thin diadem and secured her abundant brown hair, like that of the angel of the annunciation in old paintings

Her large dark violet eyes, riveted upon me, were shining, immobile in their profound orbits, like the guardian lamps of tombs. A distant light flowed into me via that gaze, a long remembrance of an ancient life, and I saw in the depths of those eyes fleets scattered over the seas and armies engulfed under the sands.

I took a long time to find my words; the sound died in my mouth. Finally, I said: "My eyes have never seen your face, but my soul knows you. Who are you, you who resuscitate dead things in my heart?"

"You know very well, since you have come," said her grave voice, which vibrated like the profound string of a viol under the bow. "I am the one who remembers; I am the one who waits. For centuries I have been looking out for the return of the Beloved to the hall of the ancestors. Their bones sleep in the crypts; their shades have fled on the winds; but I am alive because I love, and because I love, I believe."

The voice that pronounced those rhythmic words spread out within me like dew, but the presentiment of a superhuman happiness was crossed with the anguish of losing it. The speech stopped on her lips like the sound of a Aeolian harp when the wind stops blowing.

Impetuously, I said: "Will you tell me the name of your Beloved? I want to bring him to you in order to see your joy."

She smiled sadly as she put down her embroidery. She placed her elbow on the table and let her head fall upon her slender, tapering fingers. Her temples seemed to hollow out, her eyes sunk more deeply into their orbits and her gaze reached further into the distance.

"I am," she said, "the last of my race, and he is the last of his. I have received the ring. The farewell kiss is burning on my hand; tears have consumed my heart. He departed with the crusaders, the man I loved. Why has he left me in anguish? Dead or alive, it is necessary for him to return, one day. But if my soul is dead, if my knight no longer remembers, then my soul also will die in the silence...die forever. That is the punishment of those who love too much."

"Your name! What is your name! I stammered

"My name? I have forgotten it. It will be effaced with my shade if the man I love finds me again. I was the Fiancée of amour, I am the Abandoned, and I will be the Phantom Bride if I do not become the Eternal Wife."

Her voice had become almost imperceptible. The dying sounds were lost in distant spaces. I was suffering from an inexpressible pity and impotence. As in a nightmare, I strove to lift up the mountain that was oppressing me, but I remained crushed beneath its weight. It was impossible for me to remember, impossible for me to pronounce a syllable. Slowly, I saw the windows, the drapes and the chatelaine paling. Soon, her image was completely effaced. Through the fog, however, a pale hand bearing a ring on the ring finger was extended toward me. I seized it and I felt, with a warm fluid, the invasion of a torrent of memories. Then I rediscovered speech in order to cry out: "Berthe, my fiancée, is that you?"

"It's me, Konrad"—and her suave voice palpitated with profound passion—"the centuries are no more; it is the hour of Eternity."

With those words she reappeared, standing in a festival light. I saw her float rather than walk toward a dresser. She took an ebony casket from the dresser, drew closer to me and removed a crown of myrtle from the casket. With a feverish haste, her agile hands wove the green branch into her somber tresses. Her hands quivered in her curls; her cheeks on fire, she gazed at me with dilated eyes; at that moment, they were like two great thoughts; from their violet depths a golden gleam, a gleam of solemn felicity filtered over me. No woman of flesh had ever been more alive. The past and the future were engulfed in that absolute presence.

Silently, our hands met for the great betrothal.

Then, among the tapestries, under the obscure vault, the murmur of a crowd ran, like the sound of foliage agitated by the wind. In the blink of a eye, the hall was filled with people in outdated costumes. Candles were lit in the chapel at the rear. My fiancée and I found ourselves facing a great stone bishop standing before an altar. Celestial songs resounded. The stone bishop, becoming animated, pronounced the austere words of the Latin mass, which were mingled with angelic voices. Finally, raising a finger, he said: "Exchange rings; I will unite you."

I saw Berthe detach her gold ring, and I had withdrawn mine in order to pass it over the finger of the mystic fiancée...but I stopped, chilled by something terrible.

To the right of the bishop, between the altar and me, a frightful beast was crouched. From the leonine body of a sphinx protruded, immodest and proud, the torso of a woman, of a mat and sinister whiteness. The opulent and swollen breasts offered their blood-colored fruits. The arrogant and massive head was that of a Roman Empress, with a domineering profile, a powerful and sensual double chin and a helm of yellow hair pulled back from the forehead. The pink blood that was beginning to circulate in that alabaster body made the hide quiver and made the golden tufts of the nape bristle.

I sensed with terror the animal part of my being seized by the sphinx, as if the stone were drinking my blood in order to become living flesh. I experienced simultaneously the horror of the beast and the savage desire to tame or to be felled by her. A greenish aura was spread around her russet head. She turned toward me with a evil smile and launched a gaze from her little eyes more piercing than a dart.

My will fled like a river falling into a gulf. I uttered a desperate cry. Another responded to it: that of my fiancée. It had the strident sound of a harp ripped in the high-pitched strings. I threw myself toward her in order to embrace her, but I only grasped a shred of the violet robe, which remained in my hand. The candles were extinguished. I shivered in the darkness of a empty hall, in which the monumental sphinx arched her back in the glow of a dying fire, while two menacing eyes shone under a high miter in the depths of the chapel.

Then the walls of the old castle cracked. It crumbled, ripped apart by the tempest, an infernal ride carried me away like a hurricane; behind me dogs were yapping; in front of me the sphinx was galloping, her head turned to look back over her rump, mocking me with subtle laughter; around me were a herd of red deer. And we went at a frantic speed, cutting through the oaks, breaking the forest...

At that moment I woke up, covered in cold sweat. The shrill cry of a cock rose up in the silence of first light. I was lying in ferns, in the shelter of honeysuckle. My horse was grazing tranquilly in the ditch a few paces away. In front of me, the arch with the closed worm-eaten door closed the entrance to the stairway, and over my head a castle in ruins pitted the gray dawn with its disemboweled tower.

There was no more doubt about it; I was at the Castle of the Seven Winds. With a slow and sure hand, with long detours, destiny had conducted me in spite of myself to the accursed place, from which a secret dread had always kept me away. And now, without knowing it, I had gone to sleep in the redoubtable ruin. The invincible attraction that I had felt for the cousin of my ancestors was explained now; he and I were the same person. Konrad von Felseneck was Konrad von Staufen, reborn in the flesh for the ineluctable expiation.

A strange, absurd thing. Could I believe it? Surprising, impossible in appearance, everything was explained thereby: the bizarre impressions of my childhood; the pure inspirations of the adolescent, soon submerged by tyrannical male passions; and finally, the equivocal duplicity of my being, the Hell of my damned soul, riveted by its impure intoxications to the body of Woman, and yet transported in its ecstasies toward the heaven of saints and mystical brides.

Rupertus was right, then! He had divined the truth. How well he had been able to read in the obscure leaves of my heart, in the abysm of the past and the arcana of the future! So the distant shadow that he had seen wandering in the confines of my sphere was a living soul! As he had predicted, she had come, the mystical bride. The eternal Abandoned was the invincible Faithful. She had found the strength to pierce my darkness. It was her who had searched for me through the thick veil of the senses, in order to extract me from the fatal circle...

Energies of the unfathomable soul, powers of remembrance! Without having seen her in this life, I had recognized a face already loved. The beauty of her eyes and the profundity of her gaze opened another world to me, immense and marvelous, and the joy of that magical recognition had poured into my heart an ineffable certainty.

But what, then, did the monster signify that had come to interpose itself between her and me? What did the wild beast with the feminine upper body—the beast ornamented with her carnal lures, her claws and tresses, a helm of revolt and immodesty—want with me? Alas, that monster vomited by the matrices of invisible nature, more redoubtable than all courtesans, was my evil past and my baleful present; and perhaps it presaged a future more terrible still! Was the sphinx about to rush upon me and labor my flesh? Was it going to hollow out a more unbridgeable gulf between me and the person for whom I had been searching all my life? Had I recovered the guardian fiancée miraculously, only to lose her irrevocably?

At that thought, remorse, terror and horror if myself seized me by the throat. One idea remained to me: to flee, to flee that accursed place, that castle of dementia, where the she-demon had emerged from the angelic vision like a hairy caterpillar from a white and perfumed rose.

"Fool that I am!" I cried, standing up. "Phantoms of a sick brain, all that! Dreams are, after all, only dreams, mist that the morning wind chases away. Let the crypts collapse, let the bones in the ancestral sepulchers be pulverized; let us leave the ruins to crumble over the ruins, generations to chase one another and races to fall, one soul at a time, into the night of oblivion! Let us leave the dead to bury the dead and the past to sleep with the past. Long live life! Nothing is true but the present moment, ardent and unique!"

While I spoke, however, I gazed at the worm-eaten door and the dilapidated façade, where the long tresses of ivy were suspended. A nameless pity, a black sorrow, filtered through those walls. I lay down in the long grass, my head tilted back and my arms extended, my eyes fixed on the disemboweled tower as if upon the image of my life. And I remained motionless, fascinated by my fear.

Finally, the first ray of sunlight pierced the thickness of the beeches that overhung the ditch with their age-old vault and made a rampart of eternal verdure for the castle in mourning. Thousands of diamonds lit up in the grass around me. Then I got up for the second time and I shook off my nightmare with the dew from my cloak. I seized the vigorous neck of my horse. What joy to touch a living being, with hard muscles and warm blood! I launched myself into the saddle and pricked both spurs. My horse climbed the embankment of the ditch again like a goat, in three bounds, and we departed at a gallop over hills and valleys, burning the sand and whipped by the branches.

I only stopped two hours later, in the heart of a vast fir-wood. The Castle of the Seven Winds had disappeared a long time ago behind the wooded ridges. I was in the profound shade where stray sunbeams made golden patches on the carpet of moss. I could only hear the buzzing of flies in the steeples of the fir-trees, warmed by the ardent sun, and the quiver of the breeze in the resinous needles...

Gradually, the blood that was beating in my temples calmed down. The sphinx had disappeared; she had plunged underground. By contrast, the flower of my dream, the celestial fiancée, surged forth before me, luminously...and she was more than a dream! Already, she was living within me and around me, invisible but real, impalpable but ever-present, the substance of my life and the essence of my thought. Already I knew that she would be, by turns, my consolation and my judge, my recompense and my condemnation, my day and my night. And thanks to her, I witnessed the efflorescence of a new soul within me. Was it not the soul that had been germinating in my obscure consciousness since a tender age? But it had required the breath of the Other to make it bloom. Now I had the certainty of it: that Other existed somewhere; she knew me and loved me from the depths of her silence, as inaccessible as a diamond citadel.

I do not know how long I remained immobile, lost in my thoughts, while my horse grazed the green shoots of young fir trees. I respired the chaste and savage perfume of solitary flowers, white and blue flowers. They constellated in the shadow the sanctuary of the forest. And I sensed a pure breath slide into the depths of my heart like a fluid kiss. Never had I felt such happiness.

Then I heard words pronounced distinctly inside myself:

"This is the Voice of Silence. Now listen!"

I returned to Felseneck in an almost incomprehensible state of serenity, so much did it contrast with my fever and may habitual dejection. My soul, transfigured above itself, rediscovered the most beautiful dreams of adolescence, with a sort of virile maturity; for I divined its range now. In resuming the series of the events of my life I discovered their meaning and their connection. The dream of the Castle of the Seven Winds had ignited in the very heart of my darkness a redoubtable light, perhaps of salvation.

An unexpected message that I received shortly thereafter took my spirit all the way to the degree of exaltation in which great resolutions become necessary.

One morning I was rereading the chronicle of the crusades in the low room of the castle when I heard the watchman's trumpet sound three times. That signal announced a stranger. Soon, an unknown squire brought me a letter whose red seal bore a Maltese Cross. I opened it and shivered on seeing that it was signed: *Wilfried.* That name reminded me of an almost-forgotten incident of my first free years. Coming to find me at that moment it struck me with the imperious sound of a call of destiny, a voice of God.

In my foolish youth I had only had companions in pleasure. I had frequented them without liking them, and their society brought me slowly to scorn for myself, for I soon sensed that I had become similar to them. Then I took refuge in the solitude of my castle, in order to rediscover in my memories or my hopes the shreds of my torn-up being. In none of my friends had I found a veritable brother in arms, any more than I had found a leader in whom to believe, a cause to defend or a war to sustain.

Once, however, I had encountered that brother, but so fleetingly that I had almost forgotten him. It was in a *toist*, or grand tourney. The knights were divided into two troops and simulated a battle. We had all fallen from horseback, the combat continued on foot. I had overturned my adversary, who was asking for mercy, while my neighbor was at odds with an unknown knight in black armor with his visor lowered. He succeeded in overcoming him and cried: "State your name and ask for mercy!"

"Never!" replied the other, in a muffled voice.

I saw that my companion, irritated, was about to do his proud victim a bad turn, and, seized by pity for the unknown man, I said to my friend: "Your prisoner is poor, mine is rich; let's exchange."

He consented to that. Then I said to the wounded man: "I render your liberty without ransom; come into my tent."

When he removed his helmet I perceived a thin face framed by long black hair, with sad and severe blue eyes. He told me that he was an Austrian knight and had committed a great fault in his life. Since that time he had sought death without finding it. As he hardly ever spoke he had been nicknamed Wilfried the Silent. My astonishment increased when I saw a large red cross sewn on to his gray garment. He admitted that he had made a vow to render to the next crusade. It had not yet been proclaimed. Then he had sought death by other means.

The sight and the confidences of that stranger had penetrated me with a mildness full of bitterness. In evoking cherished memories, he gave me a painful remorse.

In truth, that black knight had seemed as futile in my life as the image of my soul, that soul of old, today forgotten and proscribed, which wept over its present life. Why was I not similar to a Wilfried? But the life of the court held me by a thousand bonds. I extracted the promise from him no longer to seek death and to call upon me as a brother-in-arms when the crusade was proclaimed. He made the oath and declared to me, on his departure, that he was going to make a pilgrimage to Palestine.

Yeas had gone by when I received his message at Felseneck. I had believed him dead long ago; great was my astonishment. My emotion was augmented on reading the letter. He spoke to me about his voyage to the Holy Land and his sojourn with the brothers of Saint John at Rhodes, the desperate dense of the island against the Muslims and the lamentable exodus of the Order to Sicily. He also announced his resolution to depart for Hungary, where the war against the Turks was about to burst forth. The crusade had just been proclaimed there.[4]

He concluded thus:

The man who fights with a veritable brother-in-arms under the august symbol of the Truth, has found in advance the palm of victory. United by the same faith, the brothers in arms promise to die for one another, as they fight for the same God. In advance, through all reverses and a thousand deaths, they are part of the city in

---

[4] It is unclear what "proclamation" is intended here, as Christian "crusaders" led by John Hunyadi must have been fighting the Ottoman Turks for some time by this point in the story. Subsequent references suggest that this letter must have been received after the Turks captured Constantinople in 1453 and set forth to invade Hungary, their first objective being to capture Belgrade, to which they laid siege. Hunyadi arrived there in 1455 and tried to lift the siege, fighting a major battle in 1456.

which there is only one family, only one people and only one king of glory and amour.

Come and join the new crusaders and be my brother-in-arms. One day you saved my bodily life; let me render it to you a hundredfold by summoning your soul to the true life. Come and fight by my side.

Your brother,

Wilfried.

The distant friend named, in finishing, the small frontier town where he would be in a month and asked me whether I would be faithful to the rendezvous. As I read I had sensed the words becoming heavier, their volume and their sonority growing immeasurably. By the end, they had acquired the tone of a fanfare of war.

I got up quivering. It was the last sign announced by Rupertus "When the Angel appears who wears the bridal crown...drink her light. If you perceive the Angel, the Voice of Silence will speak to you, and if the Voice speaks to you, you will hear the warrior fanfare..." The Angel was the fiancée of my dream; the Voice of Silence I had heard in the depths of my heart in the forest; now it was the warrior fanfare that was resonating in the ear of my soul, with a letter from Wilfried. Without hesitation, it was necessary to obey.

After having fed the messenger like a lord, I sent him back with a letter that promised my arrival at the rendezvous. I had decided to quit the service of the Elector and all my worldly ambitions: a supreme means of extracting myself from the pleasures in which my will was languishing, and of accomplishing my mission.

The day that followed that resolution is imprinted in my memory, like that of my great betrothal. In that unique month of my life, Berthe spoke to me, I received signs and I heard her voice.

Often, since my return to Felseneck, I had had on awakening, the sentiment of a mysterious presence. Sometimes it was like a wing gliding in the half-light from the casement windows, sometimes a whiteness surging forth behind me, the reflection of which caressed my cheek and brushed my closed eyelid.

Twice, in the transparent slumber of the morning, which seems woven by light, I had dreamed about Berthe. I had seen distinctly her large violet eyes, flowers of dream and living thoughts, fixed upon me. By means of their long vibrations they had darted their intimate meaning into me.

The first time, she had presented me with a white rose, which I had seized avidly, and I had woken up under the intoxication of a suave perfume. The second time, she had brought me a tankard in which a wine was fulgurating as crimson as the blood of her heart, which I could see beating under her robe, as red as her lips in her pale face.

On drinking that wine I had sensed a powerful cordial running through my veins. The fleeting apparition seemed to take pleasure in the ardors of the gaze; however, every time the desire for a material embrace was born in me, she vanished. The sentiment that I retained on awakening was not that of a disappointment, but of a subtle communion with the Invisible, of a delectable envelopment.

The day after the day when Wilfried's messenger took away my oath of a brother-in-arms, I saw her again in a white robe, leaning over my bed with a bouquet of large lilies. A warmer life tinted the neck emerging from bright snowy fabric with amber. The robe, the neck and the visage were shining with nuptial splendor. She spread the lilies over my bed, and under her hands of an expert weaver, they were changed into steel armor, as brilliant as silver. She dressed me in it and I felt the gentle imprint of her two hands on my breast, and the exquisite burn of her lips on my forehead.

I awoke under that supernatural kiss as under a baptism of fire. No similar exaltation had ever lifted me up. I was mad with joy, I was intoxicated, but intoxicated in strength and in purity. I compared that unusual happiness, that intense vibration of my being, with the bitter rancors of my nights of lust, the painful drill of desire, the furious needle of jealousy, the infernal desire of the senses, in which insatiability tortures us even in satiety, where the perverse curiosity of an unknown enjoyment pursues us in the blackest disgust. Now I was as free as a bird in the air, freer than I had ever been, at peace with myself and everything. The breath of a broad universe filled my lungs. A powerful desire for struggle and action whipped my light blood, which flowed in my veins as agile as fire.

I launched myself on to my horse crying: "Let's go recover Rupertus's ring!"

That poor ring! Would I find it at the Fay's Beech, where I had hidden it—how many years ago?—in order to preserve it from the jealous suspicions of my father? The moss of forgetfulness had had time to grow around it. It had slept in the knotty trunk throughout my foolish years; my shame and my remorse had kept me away from it then. But the presages were confirmed, the time had come to put the ring on my finger again. It would be the sign of a pact concluded with the Invisible, the oath to accomplish the divine will.

I penetrated the high beech forest that undulates at the foot of the Angel's Rock on a tempestuous autumn afternoon. Black clouds chased by a strong wind were running in the sky above the agitated trees. Whirlwinds of dry leaves traversed the paths, and gusts of wind roared in the trees like the sounds of an organ. When the sun was veiled, the profound wood suddenly darkened, and the pale trunks of the beeches resembled giant phantoms dolorously twisted by the wind; at the first ray that pierced the clouds, the forest resumed its aspect of a cathedral, the white boles looming up like majestic pillars, launching their arches in the vault of foliage.

Finally, the Fay's Beech appeared. Its large trunk still dominated the clearing. Half-stripped of its crown of branches, it only put out sparse leaves; its sap was slowly drying up. But, unvanquished in its gray bark, like an old warrior in his armor, it still resisted and bore its old wound valiantly, blocked by a stone. The moss had covered it and the wood had tightened. I had to cut into the tree with my hunting-knife in order to extract the block of sandstone.

I plunged my hand into the hollow filled with mildew, and uttered a cry of joy on touching the metal of the casket. I opened it with my little key and took out the ring; the gleam of the amethyst seemed to have augmented in the darkness.

As I passed the ring over my finger I murmured: "Soul or phantom, you, the Angel who commands, the unique Beloved, be the Eternal Wife. Hear my oath. This ring unites us forever.

I could have been before the altar, facing the priest before a living wife and I would not have had a more intense sentiment of possession in my soul. However, I was alone in the immense forest, and no one other than the storm-wind and the great curbed beeches sang at my marriage.

What happened within me then? What transport of pride extended as far as breaking the fibers of my being? It seemed to me that the cross was already flamboyant on my breast, and that I wore on my forehead like a star the kiss of the invisible fiancée. The clouds were bounding in the sky like cavaliers and accumulating like armies on the march. The spasmodic gusts of wind were as strident as shrill fanfares. Above the beeches, the sheer rock appeared from which people said that an angel had once preached the crusade to enthusiastic crowds.

Truly, I became someone else. Konrad von Staufen was reborn in me. A crusader breath inflated my chest and made the horizon undulate like a stormy sea. In the insensate joy of anticipated triumph, I challenged all the powers of the earth and provoked all the demons of the forest.

My horse appeared to be subject to the fever of my thoughts. As if it heard the warrior trumpet, it whinnied and was carried away. I let it run, assuming that I would reach the Angel's Rock by going around the mountain.

Suddenly the aspect of the forest hanged; the beeches gave way to meager and bare fir trees; the tender mosses to landslides with fantastic forms. At a frantic gallop my horse went along a climbing path toward an overhanging rock of sinister form.

We arrived in a higher pat of the mountain, where a small black lake with greenish reflections slumbered among the somber fir-groves. Pale reeds with morbid nenuphars bordered its banks. I understood that my frightened animal, instead of bearing me to the Angel's Rock, had passed through the wood to the Devil's Rock, drawing me all the way to the solitary and ill-famed place known as the Undines' Lake.

Discontented, I turned the bridle and retracted my steps. I had already lost sight of the lake and my horse was going back down the narrow path between the stones and the firs when a mocking and lascivious voice came to strike my ear with a gust of wind. It was so faint and so distant that it seemed to be filtered by the crystal of a wave at the exit from an unknown gulf. I distinctly heard the words of an ancient song that I had heard before:

> *You who are returning from the crusades,*
> *Ha ha! Why search for your people?*
> *Ha ha! Your beauty is no longer here.*
> *But under the lake, handsome comrade,*
> *Under the green and transparent surface,*
> *The arm of a girl*
> *A glistening breast,*
> *Awakens your heart! The Nixie is there!*
> *Ha ha!*

I had stopped, and I said in a loud voice: "Silence, cursed voice!"

An arpeggio of crystalline laughter, which seemed to come from the depths of the water responded to me. Furious I spurred my horse. It reared up over the abyss with a plaintive whinny, and malevolent fir-needles whipped my face.

IV. The Sphinx

I could not depart for the army of the Danube without the permission of the Count Palatine. I had served in his court for ten years, and I pleased him. That old lord, who enjoyed life cheerfully, loved passes of arms and dancing, music and amorous couples. Bathed in a festival atmosphere, he rediscovered his youth in gazing at his guests through the rosy vapors of wine, like a moving tapestry always agitated for his eyes. He was gripped by affection for me and pardoned my black moods because of my impetuosity in tourneys and pleasures. I had to present myself before my suzerain and obtain his permission to go on crusade.

The evening when I arrived in Spire I learned that there was a fête at the palace. I went in and found the great hall festooned with verdure and flowers. Under the sonorous vaults, dances were knotted to the sound of viols and oboes. As was his habit, the Count Palatine was sitting at the back on a kind of platform, dominating all his guests at a glance. He was chatting with two grave ecclesiastics with delicate features and penetrating eyes, while following the evolutions of the dance. Enormous drinking-vessels of silver and multicolored Bohemian glass ornamented the table set up before those individuals.

Among the vessels, a bizarre being was stirring and agitating, whose head scarcely surpassed the tallest of them; that was the dwarf Kunz, the Elector's adored fool. With his thickset body, his enormous hump and his large head, sunk between shoulders that were too broad, the little monster gave the impression of a malicious devil. Complete liberty of gestures and words was permitted to him. He was removing and replacing his bonnet, which was fitted with little bells, and he was striking the tankards of all those who came too close to the table with his bauble. His nose resembled a trunk, his chin was pointed, and his basilisk eyes, sparkling with malevolence, seemed to want to delve into all consciousnesses.

When I had announced to the Count Palatine my resolution to depart for the crusade, the fool scoffed: "Knight, for your ingratitude you merit a hundred strokes of the bauble, and for your fine project here's my fool's bonnet."

"Shut up," said the Count, "and let me speak first. Friend Konrad, you afflict me. You want to quit the best of masters in order to die of hunger or get yourself killed under the walls of Belgrade? And I wanted to make you my chief squire! You're running toward a stupid life and a bad end. Don't you know that crusades are no longer fashionable? What, then, is driving you?"

"A wish of childhood, a dream of youth, and a secret order that cannot be revealed to anyone but which I must obey like the voice of God."

"Be free then, ingrate child, and may the God of battles protect you, knight of chimeras! As the proverb says: Better a savage falcon on the wrist than a flighty friend in the heart. Before departing, however, it's necessary that you do me one favor, which is to salute my cousin, Gertrude von Hohenstein, who is presently the ornament of my court. She is the beauty of beauties and the queen of widows. You can't refuse her a game of chess or a dance."

"I don't know her," I said, indifferently.

"But she has seen you several times, and would like to know you, Konrad—and what Gertrude wants arrives, sooner or later."

"Yes," said the dwarf, "She possesses dazzling tresses, a marvelous castle and two dead husbands, with as much wit as is necessary to find three more and put them in accord or rid herself of them."

"Serpent's tongue, don't speak ill of the jewel of my family!"

"At least let him know the story of the Siren of the North before confronting her!" sang the fool.

"There isn't a word of truth in all that you're going to say," said the Elector—but at the same time, his rubicund and jovial face encouraged the dwarf with a fond smile.

At that moment my ears were irritated by a guitar *pizzicato*, mingled with the joyful laughter of men and women. They departed from the other side of a curtain that separated the back of the hall from a gaming cabinet reserved for the prince's most intimate friends. The closed curtain did not allow anything to be seen of what was happening in the little sanctuary of gamblers and gallants.

The dwarf, still standing on the table, struck a majestic pose. His elbow supported on a gigantic tankard, he started speaking, illustrating his narration with eloquent gestures.

"The bells of my bauble say more about the hearts of men than all the counselors of the Empire. Listen, then, Lord von Felseneck, to the singular history of the widow von Hohenstein. Frisian mariners captured a Danish pirate ship; in the depths of the hold a little girl was asleep among iron breastplates and golden vases, her hair coiled around a mandolin. The mariners sold her to an English lord, who adopted her as his daughter. Tossed by the waves or riding the roads, on the bearskin of adventurers or the carpet of kings, the white siren with the golden hair manipulated the hearts of men more easily than ivory balls; the child stolen by pirates was a born stealer of souls.

"A young Scotsman married her. Seeking fêtes and merriment, Gertrude took her husband to the court of France. There, playing with her fan, her eyes and her voice, she maddened the jealousy of the poor Scottish baron. He was killed in a duel by a fortunate rival. Gertrude went on her joyful way from court to court. Soon she married the Graf von Hohenstein, a distant cousin of our gracious lord, and suddenly changed her humor and her life. This time she seemed to love with a unique and jealous amour. She had the lord construct a garden of delights on the edge of a lake at the foot of the Castle of Hohenstein, and the noble lady retired there with her husband. Six months later, it was learned that the Graf, on emerging from the mysterious grotto where Gertrude, it was said, combined the art of forbidden sensualities with the art of dark magic, had drowned himself in the lake."

"Why?"

"Ask the forests, the grotto and the black swans of the lake of Hohenstein. Perhaps they know. But see how precious and rare my lord's cousin is! Her first husband died of her infidelities, her second succumbed to her constancy. What will she do with the third?

"Perhaps he'll kill her." I said, tranquilly.

Crystalline laughter from behind the curtain made me shudder. It resembled that of the undine that I thought I had heard in the depths of the green lake near the Devil's rock. I began to feel anxious.

"How does she exercise her magic power?" I asked the dwarf.

"Like this," said the fool; and he agitated the bells of his bauble around my ears. Then, giving me a great slap on the shoulder, he added in his sibilant voice: "Have you understood? Kunz is only a poor ignorant fool, but this is what people say: Gertrude is a woman in appearance but something of a she-demon deep down. To those who marry her she gives an enigma to solve, and that enigma is herself. She kills those who don't divine it, and those who divine it kill themselves. But by the blessed Saint Anthony, who resisted all temptations, like your servant, I'm weary of my prologue; I'm thirsty! Give me something to drink!"

The dwarf with the lubricious eyes emptied a tankard almost as tall as himself, and the Elector, after having moistened his lips in his glass, added: "Well, what do you say to that woman?"

"Nothing, lord, except that I have no curiosity to see her, and I ask you for the mercy of my leave."

"You're afraid then?"

"Faith of a knight, I'm not afraid of anyone. That tale is a fool's dream, and that woman has never existed except in a head coiffed in a bonnet with bells.

The dwarf rolled like a ball from the table to the floor. His clenched fists seized a silk cord running along the curtain. His yellow face, his eyes his hump and his legs were all laughing at the same time. He tugged the cord, crying: "Well, look!"

The curtain of the cabinet moved aside and revealed an elegant and bizarre trio. Two men sitting face to face were playing chess silently; they were seen in profile. The one on the left was dressed in the Spanish style in a black velvet doublet. From his lace ruff emerged a thin face with a hooked nose and a pointed chin. He had the sad expression of a bird of prey on the lookout, following his game with a profound attention. Opposite him, a young man in a blue jacket was playing his game with a distracted petulance. He often tugged his long dull blond moustache, which fell over fat sensual lips. The large nostrils of his snub nose sniffed the perfumes that were floating in the air. His prominent eyes were wandering from right to left, and his faun's ears were drinking the whining sounds of a guitar placed on his knees, which he was plucking covertly.

Suddenly, I was chilled to the roots of my hair and all my blood flowed away from my heart. Between the two players, on the other side of the table, a watchful woman was sitting, a beautiful and sinister huntress. Her face stood out, fully illuminated. I took her at first to be a creation of my inflamed brain or a diabolical apparition. I had recognized, feature for feature, the face of the sphinx!

The prophetic dream of the Castle of the Seven Winds took shape before my eyes, in a princely fête, and became a terrible reality. It really was that imperial and Byzantine visage, beneath the yellow aureole of hair drawn back in a warrior helm, but more svelte, as if rejuvenated. The fabulous beast with the bare breasts and the claws of a lioness reappeared as an elegant lady of the court clad in green velvet edged with sable. She was slowly agitating a peacock-plume fan, shining with steely flecks, over her breast. Her head was leaning slightly over the opulent and flexible neck. A disdainful smile creased the corners of her mouth.

She seemed to be plunged in an intense meditation, but she was observing her companions and her surroundings at the same time. Her pale blue eyes unleashed their oblique darts in all directions, while a comb gemmed with emeralds, securing a chignon, glinted like a green flame in her red hair. Two gilded candelabra placed on the table framed that queen of the world, brilliant with irony and crowned with audacity, like a chapel of rest.

I had clutched the flap of the curtain. A strange terror, mingled with sensuality, streamed all the way to the depths of my entrails. I gazed, fascinated, at my nightmare, incarnate in that superb woman. I experienced an anguish, and an irresistible curiosity: was she about to move and to speak to me?

"Check and mate," said the knight in black velvet, while the blond man, beaten and furious, swept the pieces from the chessboard with a thrust of his elbow.

"You felled my soldiers in vain," the victor continued, coldly. "I've won the battle. Our camp judge, Lady von Hohenstein, is the witness. Now. my lady, will you grant me the right to wear your colors in the next tourney?"

"Oh, not yet," said Gertrude, sketching a mocking smile, in a voice cadenced by the swaying of her fan. "I give a good point to Lord Hunold and engage Lord Hartwig to take his lessons. But you know very well, sires, that I only grant the right to bear my colors to the man who can beat me at chess. You've attempted the adventure but you don't have the strength. So, patience and better courage! Your hand trembles and your thoughts are troubled when our ivory armies face one another. What would happen, then, on a real battlefield? I seek an adversary without weakness and without fear; but decidedly, I despair of finding him."

"Here's Lord von Felseneck. He's burning to measure himself with you, and I'll wager that he's worthy of it!" cried the dwarf, brandishing his bauble. "Attention, over there, messires of the Holy Empire. Open your eyes and your ears; this evening, Kunz the fool will give you a comedy."

At those words the lady stopped her fan abruptly and made a slight movement. The emerald cluster glittered on her head, and her eyes, assembling their scattered radiance, transpierced me like drills. Her expression had changed by virtue of a sudden magic. A siren fluidity played over her face, and, turning toward me, in a soft and slightly veiled voice, she said:

"Approach, Lord Konrad von Felseneck; for a long time, a very long time, I have heard talk of you, and it seems that we are destined to become friends."

That smile and that sober tone rendered me the sentiment of reality. I was no longer confronting the sphinx dreamed in the Castle of the Seven Winds, but Gertrude von Hohenstein, the amiable widow and cousin of the Elector. I replied in the same tone, with a residuum of suspicion: "Very gracious and very noble lady, if I can believe my presentiment, you appear to me rather as a charming and redoubtable enemy."

"An enemy?" she said, inclining her head with a languid grace and a feigned humility. "Yes, if esteem, admiration and solicitude are enemies. Would a woman be your enemy because she desires to compete with you in courtesy and gallantry? And if, in that combat, she lays down her arms in advance, happier in defeat than in victory, would she be so redoubtable? I make you the judge of it, you who are called the most liberated knight of the Rhine and the falcon of the Black Forest. Oh, have no fear of my light arts, which are wrongly reproved, and my child-like heart, of which everyone is unaware. Sit down opposite me and let's play a game of chess. When Lady von Hohenstein surrenders to Lord von

Felseneck, he will recognize, I hope, that she is not an enemy."

I sat down, enveloped by her words. The two gallants looked at me with surly expressions. Gertrude said to them: "I have to talk to Lord von Felseneck and the Elector about the affairs of the Holy Empire. Go and rejoin the beautiful young women who are looking out for you anxiously for the dance; and later, I will dance a pavane with you, Hunold, and a pastorelle with you, Hartwig."

As they did not appear to want to go, she extended her bare arm, emerging from a long fur-edged sleeve and showed them the hall from which sounds of the viol and the flute were coming, with joyous dance tunes, sung in chorus by feminine voices. Gertrude's head inclined with a gracious gesture. Then the two chess-players got up, linked arms and drew away, darting a scornful glance at me. Their sudden hatred for me seemed to have made two friends of them.

Gertrude placed her elbow on the table and leaned her head on her hand, in a pensive attitude.

"Let's begin," she said; and with a light finger, she advanced a pawn. I did the same. Her provocative eyes harassed me.

"You've never done me the honor of intruding yourself to me, Lord von Felseneck," Gertrude continued, in her insinuating voice, "but I've known you for a long time. How many times I've observed you from behind a fan or a veil! For we have both traveled a great deal in the Holy Empire. Do you remember a fête in Augsburg at the Episcopal Palace? A column separated us, but I saw you. You were talking to the wife of a margrave, whose colors you wore then. That day, you covered yourself with blood and dust for her at the tourney, and then you asked her, in very humble and very ardent language, for I know not what favor. And the circumspect margravine said to you: 'When we permit a knight to serve us, we pull a veil over our thoughts with one hand and lift the end of it with the other...' And I, being compassionate, felt sorry for you with all my heart, Lord Konrad. She was so heavy and so stupid, the poor margravine! And her virtue seemed as solid as her majestic cheeks!'"

"You have too much pity for my sex, Gräfin, and not enough for your own."

"What do you know about it? But you're playing badly. I'm taking your bishop with my queen. Listen to a more pathetic adventure. There was a carnival in Cologne. A brunette Bohemian, a splendid young woman, was dancing around a fire. Grotesque masks flocked to watch her. Among them was a knight with his face uncovered, standing apart—that was you—and a masked lady in the company of several lords. The Bohemian had noticed the feverish attention of the knight. At the end of the dance, she leaned toward him amorously. The knight asked her for a rendezvous. She asked him for a pledge. He gave her his gold chain. The Bohemian seized it avidly, and her white teeth sparkled in the expansion of her smile like the pips of a split pomegranate. Why, then, did the Bohemian not come to the rendezvous?"

"Are you sure that she did not come?"

"Quite sure. The masked lady sent her two gold chains heavier than the knight's, and had her dance all night in her palace."

"The masked lady was you, then? You've explained a mystery. You're as cruel as you are savant. But why would the Lady von Hohenstein protect the virtue of a stranger and a Bohemian?"

"That's my secret. Be on your guard, then, you aren't playing well. Your rook is in check; I'm taking it; that's good war."

She continued in a low voice, a mysterious whisper: "I know even more about your unfortunate amours, my fine knight, my morose hawk of the great woods. It's said that you love the nixies and the undines, that you pursue them without ever embracing them, in your savage rides in the depths of the woods. It's even said that they sometimes appear to you on the edge of sinister lakes and solitary mils…but then they frighten you and you flee…you flee unsatisfied…and you only hear their mocking laughter in the depths of the water. Is that true?"

The same crystalline laughter that I had heard behind the curtain vibrated in Gertrude's beautiful throat and made me shiver. By means of what satanic spell had that woman divined my most hidden secrets? By means of what evil second sight did she read perverse thoughts in the depths of the soul? She had raised her imperious head and was observing me with her pale eyes, abyssal eyes from which a vertiginous gaze emerged. They were both troubling and piercing. Their pupils resembled the little holes that travel over the surface of dangerous rivers; the water swirls furiously around them, and once a swimmer is dragged into the funnel, he plunges into the whirlpool. I had a movement of revolt and anger against the power that was invading me. Turning away, I exclaimed: "I forgot the nixies and the undines a long time ago. Let's finish the game. Check to the queen."

All my will reverted to the chessboard. She threw herself against the enemy with a lucid and concentrated fury. I launched my two knights forward, and my bishop after them. I harassed the king and queen with an attack so abrupt and so violent that in three minutes my opponent was beaten. Finally, I drew breath, my heart swollen with pride. Gertrude smiled maliciously and watched me from the corner of her eye. She was triumphant in her defeat, and, with her head inclined over her fan, she murmured:

"You see, Gertrude the proud and indomitable is vanquished by surprise. She surrenders. Another woman would never forgive you, but I'll do more than forgive you; I'll grant you a favor that a hundred knights have requested in vain: the right to wear my colors in the next tourney.

I stood up, with a strong resolution.

"You do me a great honor, vey beautiful and very powerful lady, but the extreme joy that I would obtain from it is forbidden to me. More serious combats summon me; I'm departing tomorrow for the crusade in Hungary. I've promised a living man, I've promised a dead woman, and I've sworn to God and my own heart. Please deign to accept my homage and my adieu."

Her eyes darted an oblique glint at me, a true stiletto-thrust. However, she collected herself, seemed to meditate momentarily, and caressed her face with the peacock feathers of her fan, and then said: "So it's true, Lord von Felseneck, that you want to depart? You've beaten Gertrude von Hohenstein at chess, and you have no desire to defend her on the closed field? Adieu, then, and good crusading on the Danube. Valiant crusader as you are, you will find everywhere the Bohemian who dances and the nixie who sings. But one only encounters *the* Woman once in one's life. Adieu, my knight!"

That speech was pronounced in a slow and profound voice. I bowed; her gaze brushed me again; it was like a dart more subtle than the others. I carried it away in my quivering flesh, already bristling with her darts. As I returned to the Elector's table I heard Gertrude's voice summoning her page:

"Don't forget, the mandolin, tomorrow at noon, under the arch of roses in the garden near the fountain."

After saluting the Elector I returned to my lodgings. The window of my chamber looked directly over the Rhine. On seeing its waters shine, silvered by the moonlight, it seemed to me that I saw my life flowing before me. Like the river, it was coming from afar, from an ungraspable source, to end in the Ocean, the Unknown and the Formidable. But what were its Law, its Truth and its Goal? Like the river, I had had my stagnant waters, my whirlpools and my rapids. Like the river, I had been driven back by reefs, trying to move back toward my source and overflowing my banks. But behold: invincible fatality brought me back to the gravel of my bed, traced in advance.

And yet, thanks to Rupertus, thanks to the Angel that had leaned over me in my sleep and thanks to the Voice of Silence that had sprung from the sanctuary of my soul, another world had been unveiled. I had heard the promised fanfare, and, in taking the cross, I had glimpsed boundless liberty by way of suffering and combat. Thus raised above myself, I was going to dam the river of my life and redirect it and redirect it to my will. For I had understood the Law, the Truth and the Goal, and I had wanted them.

What, then, was the monster that was plunging me back into the midst of turbulence? Alas, it was the announced and now present seductress, the accursed and desired Sphinx, secretly dreamed but unexpected. The women I had known were only feeble accomplices. This one was living desire, the incarnation of my culpable curiosity, the woman complete in the attraction of the flesh and the science of evil. Already, her will was over me by virtue of the projection of her charm...

Well, no! She would not reckon with me!

I wanted to pray before the open window. I invoked the Angel, the invisible Fiancée. Alas, it was impossible for me to seize her diffuse image and fix my thought upon her. My prayer did not want to rise; it did not spring from the depths of my being. I went to bed.

Then, it was the Other who came, from the depths of the night, from the gulf of the shadow. She showed herself by turns under the fabulous aspect of the sphinx and the gracious visage of Lady von Hohenstein, in her costume of a huntress. She smiled behind her peacock-plume fan, making her eyes emit sharp darts. And desire, a frantic desire, increased with my hatred. It was the ancient desire to penetrate, to embrace and possess the feminine mystery, but it was exasperated, concentrated now on a single woman, who seemed to summarize the charms of others in her centuple power.

Finally, I sat up in bed, my fists clenched, crying: "I want to know who you are!"

But the sphinx mocked me with her multiple forms. The night passed in that insomnia. I had commanded my horse for the morning. At dawn I was unable to get up; my heart was leaden, I was nailed to my bed. It was broad daylight and I was still dreaming.

At noon, I went involuntarily to the Elector's garden. The air was heavy, not a leaf was stirring. An ardent sun was burning the suffocated plants. At the end of a covered pathway, near a fountain, I perceived Gertrude lying on a bed of repose. A page sitting at her feet, on a cushion, was lightly touching the mandolin. He stole away discreetly as I approached. Motionless, leaning on her elbow, Lady von Hohenstein was gazing at me. Her entire being was condensed in a fixed thought.

At every step the attraction was stronger, and I was still advancing, I only stopped when very close, facing the Enemy. Under the trellis of roses, she seemed even more troubling than the previous evening. A yellow simarre designed her supple and opulent forms, and the gilded pallor of the light garment made the deeper yellow of her hair and the mat white of her neck and arms stand out. The flowers around her were swooning, half-dead of heat; she alone raised her proud head and did not budge. We looked at one another silently, like adversaries measuring one another.

Finally she broke the silence: "Thank you for coming to bid me adieu. I expected you. When are you leaving?"

"I don't know; but I can't leave without knowing who you are. Yes, who are you, you who resemble the most beautiful and the most frightful of my dreams? Who are you, who spy on my actions and read my thoughts? Who are you, who want to enchain my arm and my will? Who are you?"

"I am the one you hate without being able to flee, and whom you love without being able to know her."

"Oh yes! I hate you in loving you, and when I love you, that is when I hate you the most. But I also want to know you, and I shall!"

This time, she could not sustain my gaze, and turned her irritated face away.

"Go, then!" she said, in a hoarse and dull voice that I was hearing for the first time. "Go! If you are only able to hate, you had better...and go immediately."

I seized her hand, posed on the fabric. "I'll go, but I want to know the enigma."

She raised her head and with her most beautiful smile she handed me a cornelian ring, which was like a bloodstain on the nacreous whiteness of her hand.

"The enigma is here. Look at my motto on the carved stone."

"I see a siren emerging from the waves. She's holding a mirror in one hand and a harpoon in the other."

"Read what is written underneath."

I read:

Look into my mirror;
The enigma laughs in its depths.
You will know my secret
By breaking my harpoon.

"Well, she said, "if you're afraid of the siren, flee, flee quickly and flee forever..." She added, in an insinuating voice: "But if you want to decipher the enigma, you whom I seek and whom I await, if you want to possess the siren, with Gertrude von Hohenstein, then let us join our lips and our destinies. Do you want to?"

I gazed at her, trying to struggle. Her body still extended, her head and shoulders raised up toward me, she looked longingly at me with brilliant eyes, the gulfs of which seemed to become more unfathomable as her gaze plunged deeper into mine.

My hand, gently drawn, brushed her extended hand. Our fingers interlaced. The emprise was sudden and treble. Enveloped by a wave of fire, I fell to my knees, crying: "I love you!"

There was a flash of joy in her eyes. Her hands clenched on my shoulders and I had the sensation of claws digging into my flesh. Vanquished, I yielded, with the voluptuousness of an abandonment that succeeds long resistance. Drowning in a sea of delight, I allowed myself to be inundated by the effluvia falling from that powerful forehead and those eyes, and, fascinated, I followed the contour of that sinuous mouth, the lips parted with languor, in which I saw the rosy dart of a sharp tongue appear.

At that moment, my gaze brushed my own hand, captive in Gertrude's, and I saw Rupertus's amethyst shining on my finger, the ring of my mystical betrothal. Remorse shook me from head to toe. The phrase "I love you!" that I had just uttered to the siren in the pangs of desire, the phrase that engaged my life, in which my liberty sank with the higher dream of my soul, appeared to me in its blackness and its cowardice.

I closed my eyes and I believed that I saw the true Fiancée, the Angel crowned with myrtle, turn away, veiling her face. Afterwards I no longer saw anything but a violet star; it fled, diminished and was extinguished like a dot in the darkness.

Gertrude had doubtless remarked a change in my face; she took my head in her hands and covered it with burning caresses. My consciousness of the past was submerged by the flood of new sensations. But in the mad intoxication of that double seizure of possession, we exchanged challenging gazes, and our first kiss was like a bite.

A month later, I married Gertrude von Hohenstein.

V. Black Magic

The Castle of Hohenstein, where I spent the first months of my marriage, stands in a wild and solitary country. It springs like a natural pylon from a escarpment of volcanic rock, which it crowns audaciously with its massive towers.

On one side, an abyss separates it from enormous mountains, which rise vertically, and surround it with a semicircle of colossal walls, denuded peaks and somber precipices. Under the giants that protect it with an insurmountable barrier and dominate it with an eternal menace, the fortress, seemingly inaccessible, looms up like a superb challenge to nature. On the other side, the enclosure is linked by a steep fir-wood to a labyrinth of rounded wooded hills with serpentine ridges, which form a rich solitude at its foot, a garden of delights. Encased in the hollow of a valley, a small lake smiles. It shines strangely between the velvet of its grassy shores and the dense forest that encloses it like an impenetrable mystery.

The lake resembles a living eye in the earth, in which ever-mobile thoughts glide through profound depths. It is green in the morning, blue at midday and yellow and crimson in the evening. There is no hut on its edge, no boat on its surface. Black swans float there silently. In a lost cove of that lake is the grotto that Gertrude transformed into a place of enchantments and mysterious voluptuousness. From Hohenstein the entrance to the grotto, unknown to everyone and undiscoverable, cannot be seen. A single path leads there, winding around the thickness of the woods amid the tangle of hills. Beyond the mountainous and forested zone one perceives in the distance the plain, with its rivulets, villages and towns. Thus relegated to the mists of the horizon, the world of men seems unreal, while only the giant mountains, the forests and the lake are alive: dragons, chimeras and magic, which the lofty fortress commands as a capricious queen.

For a few weeks I remained plunged in total forgetfulness of my former life and of myself, uniquely occupied in intoxicating myself with the woman who enlaced me in the tortuous folds of strange sensations. My dear past, my mystical childhood, my sweet dreams and my virile resolutions had not disappeared completely from my memory; all those things continued to live in a vaporous and improbable distance, with my soul of old. When, after long days of abandonment, my will was able to reassert itself, it was concentrated on one unique point: to study Gertrude and to divine the enigma of the sphinx.

The more I possessed her body, the less I divined her soul. That soul was subtle, multiple and deceptive. It stole away. slipping between my fingers every time I thought I might grasp it, while the woman of flesh poured me the bitter and sweet wine of pleasure, caused me to buckle under the chain of her arms and wove around my senses an ever-heavier veil of perfumes, kisses and caresses.

Every night brought us to and confounded us in the same couch; I was never witness to her slumber. She went to sleep after me and awoke before. I sometimes lost consciousness in her embrace, but I could not see her swoon. On the contrary, her will seemed to be increased by the most violent sensations, and in my long weaknesses I often saw her fiery eyes suspended over my torpor. Yes, my body and my senses were vanquished, and yet, bizarrely enough, I did not experience any fear. If I did not disentangle the depths of her soul, I sensed that she was no more able to penetrate mine. Undoubtedly, there was strength and an incalculable danger in her, but there were also reserves in me: arcana that she did not suspect, and from which my intangible will might spring forth again one day.

She nicknamed me "her domesticated falcon" and I called her "the Sphinx," after my dream.

"I'm still only the Siren by my blazon; perhaps by means of you I'll become the Sphinx," she said. And her laughter fell in a silvery cascade of a mocking soprano and a pithy alto.

By day we went hunting with falcons and greyhounds in the vast forests that undulated around the castle. We almost always traveled under trees; sometimes, on a height, through a cleft in the overhanging rocks or an abrupt gap in a forest, I perceived the lake with the chameleon reflections and I tried to make her descend there. Leaning toward her ear, griped by an ardent curiosity, I murmured: "When shall I see the grotto?"

"Not yet," she replied. "It's the great marvel of my domain; it's necessary to merit it."

And, a proud and provocative huntress, she released the bridle of her horse or launched the falcon after a high-flying kite, and we followed, palpitating, the whirling combat of the two birds; finally, one of the two fell, bleeding, behind the black points of the firs into the high bracken.

One day, when I was bored and distracted, she stopped in a remote place where the tightly-packed trunks of the fir-wood made a dense shade. Several lost paths, covered with invasive grass, met at a dilapidated hut. She sent our horses with our falconers and our valets to a nearby farm and, alone, we took a primitive path through the tenebrous wood. Contrary to her habit, she was mute and pensive. Soon, the lake appeared, a somber blue under the ardent sun, behind the red trunks of centenarian pines. When we reached the shore, abruptly, we were at the entrance to a natural corridor in the living rock.

"It's there...come," she said, in a low voice. And she drew me in.

We followed several corridors, scarcely illuminated by the fissures overhead. Here and there, sculpted figures appeared, engaged in the brute stone, amorous couples or monsters writhing in the flanks of the rock. We finally reached a spacious chamber carpeted by obscure fabrics. A lamp in the form of a dragon suspended from the vault cast a vague light there. At the back we saw a royal couch, both a throne and a bed, sustained by a rearing chimera. Behind that couch, on a crimson tapestry, a trophy of javelins and halberds was shining like a pale sun. At the other end of the chamber was an oval mirror; two copper serpents framed it and crowned it with their heads. In front of the mirror a fire was brooding under ashes in a bronze cresset. On an ebony table, three green flasks were placed, and an open book.

Gertrude installed herself with a solemn languor on the throne-bed sustained by the chimera. Her lips were quivering slightly. Sinister desires lit up in her eyes. She started to speak in a soft voice.

"Konrad, you do not know me yet and you do not suspect the infinite realm of sensuality. You have only possessed women of flesh; but the figures of dreams, the larvae of the air and the inanimate shades of illustrious lovers have attractions unknown to the vulgar. Light breaths and subtle caresses emanate from those aerial forms. With them there are amours only known to magicians. Well, I can evoke those charming shades and animate them by means of my power...more than that, they enter into my body. For an hour, for a few moments, according to my desire, they choose me as a habitation; then I appear with their face, their gestures and their voice.

"Do you understand, Konrad? You can possess them in me. For there are a thousand women in me, and if you love me, it is because they please you by turns. Look over there are those golden vials. Throw the essence of one of those flasks on the fire, pronounce the words of the book, and you will see a form appear in the mirror. Fix your eyes upon it and don't take your eyes off it. When it has disappeared, return to me. My body will not have changed, but my face, my gestures and my voice will be those of the woman evoked by your desire, and, whoever she might be, if you wish, she will be yours. Would you like Konrad, to enter into the magic circle, to descend with me into the gulf of unknown joys?

"You're making me shiver," I told her. "Your lips are pale and your eyes burning. Where do you want to take me?" And I added, to myself, putting my hand on the hilt of my sword: "I want to know the enigma!"

Gripped by a heavy slumber, she had collapsed against the back of the couch without responding to me. I approached the mirror and I grasped one of the flasks. In black letters on the enamel the words *Perfume of Enid* were legible.[5] I poured the essence into the middle of the brazier. A white vapor spreads into the grotto with an odor of lavender and vervain. It exhaled all the freshness of spring; it awoke the desire for pure amours. Then I took the book and pronounced in a loud voice the first formula of vocation that was written therein:

Enid, Enid of the chaste mantle,
Emerge from the mirror as profound as the sky.

The white vapors dissipated. The mirror took on the hue of a dark green pond, scarcely transparent. In its depths, a virginal figure with blonde hair in braids oscillated as if she were emerging from a lake. Her head bowed, she seemed lost in the contemplation of a rose that she was holding in her had. Finally, she raised her head and I perceived, vaguely, her charming features and her dreaming eyes, like two water-flowers. But immediately, she paled and faded away, more lightly than a shadow. I was disappointed by her disappearance and I turned round.

How surprised I was to see Gertrude asleep! Her face had conserved its essential contours, but it was as if the features were transfigured and modeled by another soul. Bathed in a pure fluid, Gertrude resembled the young woman in the mirror. As I approached she raised herself up on her elbow, and struck Enid's pose. She too was holding a rose in her hand and gazing at it, as if it respired the perfume of first amour and innocence rediscovered. Her eyes still lowered, she said in a soft voice:

---

[5] Enid [*Enide* in French] is a character in the Arthurian romance *Erec et Enide* (c.1170) by Chrétien de Troyes

"Do you recognize this rose? I picked it by the stream, under the linden tree, on the day of the adieu. You pushed me away harshly because I had called you an idle knight, and you departed in anger. Now you've returned. It hasn't faded in my hands during your long absence, Will you refuse it again, the rose perfumed by my thoughts and opened by my sighs?"

She held out the flower to me with candid eyes and a virginal gesture that I did not recognize as Gertrude's. I observed her, arms folded, full of an ardent curiosity. A secret instinct warned me not to take the flower. Involuntarily, my eyes were blazing. Then, abruptly she brought to rose back to her breast, lowering her head. A light blush spread over her face and her eyelids veiled her eyes.

There was such a strange charm in seeing that virginal soul surge forth in the lustful and violent magicienne, like a white nenuphar in dark water, that I nearly yielded to the illusion. A contagious tenderness softened my will, but I looked at my amethyst; I had the sensation of a pure radiance filtering from the stone, which made the false virgin seem vain to me.

Without changing posture, I replied: "No, keep your flower, for I don't believe you. You're not Enid. Beneath the whiteness of our breast I can see your changing heart of a siren. If you want to attract me, show me another face."

Gertrude's body was shaken by a spasm. A rapid convulsion agitated her features, which resumed their ordinary aspect. She fell back into a lethargy on the princely couch that served as a throne for her delirium. She moaned with anguish, and then said with a profound sigh: "Evoke, evoke another woman!"

I took another flask and I spread the liquid over the embers. Thick black clouds enveloped me. They were scented simultaneously with the intoxicating perfume of roses and the bitter odor of funereal cypresses. I pronounced the second formula of evocation written in the book:

Guinevere, sweet lover, dethroned queen
Return, beautiful adulteress, to condemned tears!

After a time behind the swirls of smoke, in the utmost depths of the mirror, a woman appeared in the gray robe of a penitent. Her emaciated face, of a wan whiteness, was framed by long black hair, which hung down over her shoulders like threads of ripped cloth. Her fixed, dilated, invasive eyes were burned by fires of remorse and an inextinguishable passion. A golden circle ringed her royal forehead. The blue gauze that enveloped her head sometimes quivered under invisible caresses and sometimes twisted in a frightful wind. Her eyes were filled with tears. They trickled, like pale diamonds, down her transparent cheeks. Then, with her crossed hands, the shade drew the veil over her face, sank slowly, and disappeared, into the blue night of the mirror.

I turned round.

Gertrude, her forehead on her joined hands, had plunged her head into the cushions. I touched her shoulder. She uttered a slight cry and, raising herself up on her elbow, showed me a face as distressed and as terrified as that of Queen Guinevere.

"Is that you, my friend?" she said. "How you frightened me! Oh yes, I always waited for you, in spite of everything. But why have you come to seek me here? Go away! I'm no longer anything but a poor nun imprisoned in a convent. Go away, I'm no longer anything but a accursed woman. I've sacrificed everything for you...husband, honor, the throne and eternal salvation...everything, for the joy of enabling your desire, of loving, loving without restraint. Now I no longer have anything to give you. I no longer have anything but my withered body and my remorse. The king has been killed, his army defeated; everything has collapsed because of us. Go away, I tell you, let me weep, weep tears of blood, until the end...

"But no, don't go! Stay to defend me. The king isn't dead, he'll return again to lie in wait for me in the tower that sheltered our secret happiness. Do you hear that distant horn and the clash of weapons? They're coming to surprise us; the tower is surrounded; impossible to escape. Come, let's hide! Give me your lips before they tear me from your arms! Come and touch this veil, in which I hide my blushing face, and cover it with kisses seeking my eyes and my mouth. Now it's drenched with my tears! Come...one more hour of paradise before eternal Hell...but that hour will also be eternity!"

I listened, palpitating, and I saw the proud Gertrude felled by the terrors and intoxications of adultery. Her entire being dissolved in a sea of tears and suppliant desires. Words, gestures and gazes flowed in my veins like a mortal fluid, a poison of folly. Once again I consulted the amethyst. A light sprang from it so mild that it suddenly appeased my convulsed senses. By its piercing light, beneath the splendid woman, broken by amour and dolor, the tortuous soul of Gertrude reappeared to my eyes, and I said:

"If you were truly Guinevere, I would love you with an immense pity and an immense amour; but I see your soul radiant with sinister diamond-shapes like the skin of a viper and the venomous dart beneath your gilded tongue. You do not have your true face yet. Let's go! I want to know who you are!"

She writhed under my commandment like a trampled snake raising its head to bite, and said with a sort of gasp and hiss: "Well then, the third! Summon the third!"

I returned to the mirror and threw the liquid in the third flask on to the fire.

Crimson smoke enveloped me. It was scented with musk and sandalwood, and that odor resembled the perfume of a thousand royal women mixed with a rich incense of Oriental temples.

I pronounced the third formula from the book:

From the bloody and blue-tinted shadow,
Surge forth, pale and cruel Cleopatra.

From the nebulous mirror a terrible woman emerged majestically.

She carried a scepter surmounted by a sphinx, and for a diadem, a coiled golden serpent. Her shiny black curls, artistically interlaced, covered her temples and her cheeks with a trellis of ringlets. Her shoulders and neck had the proud curve and brown color of beautiful amphorae, but the face was pale with lust, the mouth suave, and the nostrils palpitating. The eyes, as black as night, seemed both to absorb life and to give death.

I closed my eyes, unable to support that gaze. When I opened them again, the image in the mirror had disappeared; but when I turned round, I perceived Gertrude in the attitude of the queen. Her eyes had the same blinding fixity as those of the phantasmal Cleopatra. She did not seem to see me. All her thoughts, all her powers, seemed to be concentrated on a unique point. She commenced in a low voice, slightly hoarse at times.

"Kings, Emperors and heroes have passed before my eyes. They have agonized at my feet and paled in my arms; they have melted like wax in my fiery embrace. They are no more than phantoms...but I live, ever ardent, ever unsatisfied. I am burning and dying of desire without my flesh ever dying. I am weary of blood, of male screams, of human hecatombs. Oh, that thirst for a new amour! For without it, I shall perish, consumed, frozen, withered..."

Suddenly turning toward me, with a milder flame in her eyes and her voice, she went on:

"But you, the last, the youngest, the most handsome...you, my equal in desire...perhaps you will finally satisfy me and I will enable you to live throughout my life. To you I will give all the mysteries of my being. Come and respire this languid lotus... It is death that I offer you on my bosom, the sweetest of deaths...death in amour and in voluptuousness."

Leaning forward, she seized my wrist and looked at me. This time the temptation had something irresistible, for the parent shade, incarnate in Gertrude, made her true nature spring forth. Her skin had become shinier, her pulled-back hair, as rutilant as flames, reared up like snakes. Her power seemed multiplied a hundredfold by the effluvium of her ancient peer or her anterior incarnations. I nearly fell, vanquished, into her claws, and I felt that it would be my irremediable doom. But Rupertus's ring, pressed to my forehead, saved me once again. It penetrated me with a divine remembrance and a supernatural light.

"Ah! Terrible Sphinx, Woman-Vampire! Yes, Sphinx, Sphinx, Sphinx is your name! Frightful magicienne, you attract spirits in order to don their appearance. All women seem to be incarnate by turns in you, but you have no soul, and you are afraid of dying. That is your distress and your damnation. I am beginning to understand why your lovers, maddened by your changing forms, intoxicated by your lies, steeped in your emptiness, dejected and exhausted, but not satisfied, throw themselves in the lake. You only live on the fumes of our blood and our amour. You have all the powers of intoxication and illusion, but you are only appearance and magic. You are everyone and you are no one, being nothing but a gulf. So I shall break your mirror!"

I shattered the glass into smithereens with the hilt of my sword. Gertrude uttered the strident scream of a wild beast. With a gesture as rapid as lightning, she had snatched a javelin from the trophy of weapons and, brandishing it against me, she said with an expression of fury and hatred: "Beware! You've broken the mirror but not the harpoon!"

We looked at one another, immobilized in an attitude of challenge.

I've wounded the beast but I haven't killed it, I thought—and I emerged from the grotto.

Bright afternoon sunlight fell upon the mirror of the solitary lake, which was now glittering with emerald tints. What subtle attraction was brooding in its depths? Whence came those dark or bright patches that marbled its surface, only to sink immediately? Why did red deer and roe deer flee this vicinity? Why were there no other flowers on its shores but funereal nenuphars, no other birds on its surface but black swans? Why did the beeches and the centenarian pines clustered on the edge extend their old men's arms over the water recklessly? Why did one see the pale tresses of pellitory plants drawn out so sadly here?

Yes, there was a kind of vertigo of suicide around that lake. All beings were subject to that fascination. Graf von Hohenstein must have yielded to it when, tottering and insane on emerging from the arms of Gertrude and her maddening sorceries, he had fallen from some high rock into the deep water. But I had smashed the charm, I had broken the circle of enchantment. A powerful desire was driving me now to raise myself above that heavy and burning air, to climb like a bold hunter on to the alpine heights whose peaks were staged behind the castle. I had recovered my crossbow lost in a path. I put it over my shoulder and without rejoining our retinue, leaving Gertrude in the depths of her grotto, I went to traverse the dense forest alone.

I marched in a straight line, away from the paths, cutting through thickets, crossing streams, ravines and slopes. I plunged toward the goal that I had fixed for myself: a sharp peak that emerged from the fir-wood. I attacked the wooded foothills of the great mountain and reached meadows constellated with chaste flowers swept by a fresh wind. I saw the flocks of goats and ewes disappear behind me as I entered the wild region of vultures and eagles. I finally reached the base of the peak that dominated the grassy ridges, an immense, inaccessible, naked pyramid. Hawks were soaring in circles around the summit, shining in the sunlight like flecks of silver cradled by the blue sky.

I stride along on the grass, steaming with sweat. Finally, I paused for breath; I was free! The bushy ocean of forests was lost beneath my feet; the amphitheater of the mountains was enlarged; I overlooked the maze of ravines from which I had just emerged, thanks to the vigor of my agile feet and my avid lungs. And was it not mine, the unlimited horizon of the life that I had wanted to conquer, as well as the plain displayed before me in the gray mist with its towns and rivers? Was I not about to launch myself forth again?

I extended my arms and then let them fall back, as a bird retained by its chain flaps its quivering wings. No, I was not free. Like those mountains, which formed profound ditches and enormous palisades around the lake and the solitary castle, my desires, my curiosity and my ambitions had built a triple row of ramparts around my will. Yes, I was like Rupertus's spider, attracted momentarily by the crystal globe, but which soon returned to its prison of threads expertly woven by itself. And I felt strongly that, although I had broken her magic mirror, the Sphinx still held me in her bonds. That was the punishment. It was necessary to break my chain at all costs—but how?

When I returned to the castle, an old man-at-arms was waiting for me in the courtyard, His clothes were in tatters, his helmet dented. He had the hollow cheeks and face of a man corroded by fever.

"Who are you?" I asked him.

"Lord Wilfried's squire. He died in my arms outside Belgrade and charged me with this letter for you."

I took the sheet of paper and read:

My task is accomplished. Adieu! Your brother-in-arms, who loves you. Wilfried.

So, I had forgotten him and left him alone at the crusade in order to follow the Sphinx ardently, while he, the strong and the faithful, had remembered me at the fatal hour. From the depths of death he had sent me the knight's salute. A heart unbreakable in amity as in faith, a true brother-in-arms. That simple adieu of an obscure hero overwhelmed me with all its mildness and showed me the void of my life more clearly than the bitterest reproaches. I took the messenger into the hall of the castle; we sat down in the embrasure of a window and I poured him the wine of honor myself. When he had finished giving me all the details of the death of my friend, I asked him whether the war was over.

"No," he said, "the siege of Belgrade is still going on."

"Will you depart again with me in order to guide me there?"

"I'm old and have no hearth, sire; I might as well die out there as here."

"That's good; we'll leave tomorrow."

Darkness was falling in the large hall, the columns of which were decorated with weapons and hunting trophies: the heads of red deer, ibex and wild boar. At that moment I saw Gertrude advancing toward me in the severe costume of a chatelaine, her head enveloped in a veil. I got up as she approached and we looked at one another. She said to me in a jovial voice: "Has my lord and master had good hunting today?"

"Marvelous! I've found the finest thing in the world: a companion in arms."

"This man in rags, old and worn-out? Truly, the game isn't handsome; the hunting leaves much to desire."

"He's the squire of my friend Wilfried, who has died outside Belgrade. I'm departing with him tomorrow for the Danube."

"Ah!" she said, gaily. "The forgotten crusade? That's right! Before that departure, I could ask you to take me to Felseneck. Is not your castle mine, as this one is yours? But I prefer to keep my domain, where I have a great deal to do. Leave without delay, then. You have need to respire the dust of the high roads and the odor of battlefields, in order to recover a taste for the air of hunts and amorous dalliances. When you return, you will find Hohenstein embellished by its chatelaine. As for the grotto of the lake, you're too brutal to understand its subtle magic. You can search hard, but you'll never rediscover the route to it. Access is closed to you, and the magicienne of the lake bids you adieu. Bon voyage and a fine crusade, Lord von Felseneck!"

Gertrude turned her back on me after having unleashed that dart. It did not move me; a sensed therein the chagrin of the Sphinx, divined and wounded. I sat down again in the embrasure of the window next to the sick squire, and I put my arm around his shoulder as if he were Wilfried himself.

Soon, from the terrace of the inferior stage, on to which Gertrude's chamber opened, I heard the whining sound of a rapidly plucked string instrument. The chatelaine, enveloped in a large gray mantle, was leaning on the edge of the terrace, her head inclined toward the abyss. On a stone bench beside her, her little page was playing the guitar nonchalantly and started singing songs in a foreign language, accompanied by an ironic and irritating dance rhythm.

Night had already blackened the gulfs of the forest; sinister vapors were rising in a spiral from the lake, plunged in darkness; up above, the livid peaks were draped majestically by twilight, and the crimson of the sunset was smoking like a conflagration.

For a long time yet I lent my ears to the disconnected story of the man in rags. He talked about battles, sieges, plagues and famines. In the end, I ceased to listen to what he was saying. His eyes appeared to me to be two lamps in a poor chapel; fundamentally, Wilfried was sleeping in armor in the peace of eternity...

And the page's guitar continued its mocking music, and the gray chatelaine, the malevolent sphinx, was still dreaming, leaning on the balustrade and inclined over the abyss...

When I awoke, my first thought was to have my horse saddled, my second was to run to the terrace to gaze one more time at the lake and to launch my last challenge to that place of perverse enchantments. The little page was waiting for me there with his guitar.

"Where is the mistress?" I asked him.

He linked his eyes with a languorous and malign expression.

"Gräfin von Hohenstein," he said, plucking the strings of his instrument, "departed at daybreak with her retinue. She is going to join the Prince Palatine."

"Departed? At daybreak?" I asked, astonished.

"Look out there," said the page.

He pointed to a little valley beyond the lake. In a fold in the terrain, the helmets of a troop on horseback were glinting, followed by several baggage carts. A woman was riding at the head. I recognized her hat with white plumes; it was Gertrude, I remained nonplussed, but, hiding my surprise, I said to the page: "That's good; leave me alone."

And, curbed over the gulf at the same place where, the evening before, she had leaned over, I followed the distant cavalcade with eyes dazzled by the early morning, sun until it disappeared in the forest.

How she deceived me, I thought. *What is she going to do out there?*

The torrent was roaring in the abyss, spasmodically, with demonic laughter. The colors of the lake mutated from emerald to blue. Were not the charming phantoms of Enid, Guinevere and Cleopatra, the women of old evoked in the marvelous grotto and incarnated by the magicienne, wandering there somewhere, in a lost cove? My heart was upset. The entire landscape now wove around me a network of invisible chains. It seemed to me that I could hear the monstrous portcullises of the fatal chateau falling, in order to imprison me therein.

Finally, a veritable cry of anguish escaped my lips: "What has she done to me before departing? Have I not heard the fanfare? Is it not the crusade that is summoning me? Who, then, will prevent me going to Belgrade? O gulf of woman, O labyrinth of my own heart, more unfathomable and perfidious than that lake! When the work of evil has commenced, it is necessary that it finishes. I don't know everything about the Sphinx yet; it's necessary that I follow her!"

VI. The Tourney

By tedious routes across country and through towns, from one stage to another, I had followed Gertrude. I did not appear at the Elector's fêtes, but I prowled around the palace.

One evening, Hunold, the chess-player reminiscent of an owl accosted me gravely

"Excuse me. Lord von Felseneck," he said. "I had the honor, six months ago, of being supplanted by you in a game of chess in the company of the very illustrious Lady von Hohenstein, who became your wife. But today you have been supplanted yourself in playing the guitar by my former opponent, with regard to the gracious queen of games of amour and courtesy. You are doubtless aware that Lady von Hohenstein has been here for three days? She has not wasted any time."

"What do you mean?"

"There is a proverb that says: a love letter laid on a green branch dreads the paw of a cat and the beak of a magpie. The beak of a magpie has picked up this one: Lord Hartwig dropped it in front of me at the quintain exercises."

I read on a pretty parchment scroll:

Tomorrow at midday, under the rose bower, the lady love will give her guitar lesson to the discreet knight. If he does not want to incur wrath, let him be faithful to the rendezvous.

A festoon of colored flourishes garlanded the message. At the bottom, the siren's seal was visible, with her mirror and her harpoon.

"Thank you, Lord Hunold," I replied, affecting the greatest calm and handing the letter back to him. "Lady von Felseneck is free to teach music to whomever she pleases, as I am free to give lessons in swordplay to anyone I wish."

The next day, at noon, I slipped into the Elector's garden, of which Gertrude had reserved the coolest and shadiest corner. I approached by a side-path and hid behind a hawthorn bush. Gertrude was lying on an ivory bed under the rose arbor, in the same pale yellow simarre, with the same troubling abandon, in which I had seen her myself a few months earlier. Hartwig occupied a silk cushion at her feet.

Let's see," said Gertrude, pensively. Sing me the *Lay of the Nightingale* by Walter von der Vogelweide."[6]

"On condition that you begin by giving me the key. For you are the sovereign of the joyful or sad songs of my heart."

Gertrude took the guitar negligently, played a prelude and intoned in a fresh voice the perfumed song of innocence, amour and spring:

In the heather,
Under the lindens,
Come to find me my dear friend;
In the heather

---

[6] Walther von der Vogelweide (c.1170-c.1230) was a *minnesänger* who composed many love songs, including the famous "Under den linden," of which the lines cited begin with a rough translation but then diverges markedly in order to contrive French rhymes. I have translated Schuré's version rather than substituting an English translation of the original Medieval German text.

We'll be alone
Many bouquets we have picked
In the valley very gently
Trallaradour!
Said the singing nightingale.

"To you the second verse, Lord Hartwig," said Gertrude; and she held out the instrument.

"How," said the wonderstruck gallant, "can one sing after you, who make the strings and the voice correspond as the angels of paradise do? In listening to you I sense my voice and my heart failing, and I can no longer sing.

"It's necessary, however. The mistress of music commands it. Imagine that you're a young woman dreaming about her first amorous rendezvous. Her mouth is red with the kisses she has just received; her heart is palpitating. She is crazy with fear and joy, but so amorous and so innocent that she has no suspicion of the sin committed... Let's go! It's very easy..."

Hartwig sang the second verse. He emphasized the words and the melody heavily. His violent passion was betrayed in his thick voice, and his rude singing lost the soul of the song, more delicate than a butterfly's wing and lighter than peach-blossom fluttering in the April breeze. Gertrude gazed at him complaisantly. She was visibly playing with the desire that she excited and the embarrassment of that German faun, intoxicated by the presence of a woman sovereignly accomplished in seduction.

"You don't have the heart of a young woman," she said, smiling.

And she resumed the strophe with a mysterious palpitation:

He went to make
A bed for us
Of jasmine and fresh lilac,
In the heather
Someone laughed
I'm sure of it, as they passed by
Between the roses someone could,
Trallaradour!
See where my head reposed.

"The end! The end, I beg you!" stammered Hartwig, gazing at her fondly.

Gertrude concluded, in a languid ecstasy, her head leaning over the instrument:

How many caresses
I received,
I'm still shivering with shame...
How many caresses
I returned...!

She stopped, as if suspended in her dream, and then, with a sudden rush of joy, she took up the refrain:

No one knows but my friend.
And the joyful nightingale!
Trallaradour!
Be discreet, little bird!

And she dropped the guitar with a deafening burst of laughter. Hartwig, mad with amour and struck by stupor, was fixed in place. He was doubtless wondering what there was of truth in that woman, who launched flames and shook snow around her by turns, artfully sliding a point of irony into her siren songs.

I had some difficulty remaining calm in my bush. I made a movement and I broke a branch. Gertrude started. Could she see me with her piercing eyes? Did she suspect that I was spying? Perhaps. She had shivered with pride, not fear. Her provocative speech was like a challenge addressed to me.

"Lord Hartwig, you're kneeling there like a monk praying. Are you timid, or are you afraid of Lord von Felseneck?"

At those words, Hartwig flew to Gertrude's feet like a moth to a bright flame.

"Gertrude," he said, with a sincere ardor, "let me wear your colors at the next tourney. If I steep them in my blood, will you believe in my amour?"

"Yes, I want that," she said. "You, at least, know how to give yourself!"

She looked at him with her abyssal eyes and drew him to her with both hands. It was the emprise that I knew so well, the claw of the sphinx posed on its prey. My first reaction of exasperated masculinity was to kill both of them, but I was afraid of that cowardly impulse and found myself ridiculous. I sensed, moreover, that Gertrude, insulted by me in her womanly pride, would have the right and the power to stop me with a gaze. I knew that I was defeated and I retired, meditating a more knightly vengeance.

Hiding in an inn for several days, I understood with horror that, far from extinguishing my passion, frightful jealousy had irritated it with its venom, and that my secret desire for Gertrude was sharpening my hatred and my scorn. But I hoped to finish with that deadly amour by punishing my rival and liberating myself forever from the sphinx by hollowing out a moat of blood between us.

The nights that followed have only left me atrocious memories. I marched in an ardent furnace through which provocative visions passed. I saw Gertrude enthroned there in golden gauze with her opportunistic lover, mocking my disdain. The boor embraced her; she smiled, mocking me. Then I lacerated both of them with dagger-thrusts...then, when she gasped, expiring, I repented and I covered her beautiful palpitating body with kisses. I was plunged by turns into fire and ice. Successively, in a matter of minutes, I was the severe administrator of justice, the quivering murderer and the bewildered lover. I no longer knew who I was; I had lost the government of my thoughts and I watched them flee over the swollen sea of my passions like a dismasted ship drifting helplessly.

Impetuous and fixed in the midst of those tempests, however, my will pursued its plan of vengeance.

The tourney was proclaimed. I had myself announced there as a foreign lord ad I adopted other armories. No one was aware of my presence. Only the preparations for the combat and its bloody end have remained present in my memory.

In a huge meadow in the middle of the countryside stood the palisades of the closed field and the poles with floating banners. Not far away were the tents of the combatants with their multicolored escutcheons. In mine, my valets fitted me with black armor, with a helm of the same color. I had attached a branch of cypress and myrtle to it in memory of the invisible fiancée to whom, in my profound thought and beneath the seething foam of passions, my heart remained secretly faithful. Around the tents, the horses harnessed by the squires were pawing the ground, and jugglers, tightrope-walkers, fiddlers and bone-setters were swarming, the lost children of the highway, including vagabond women with provocative gazes and garish dresses. Everywhere there were cries, banners, prancing cavaliers, and open-air forges in which fire blazed, where the bellows blew and the hammer fell upon the anvil in order to repair dented helmets and twisted swords.

Finally, the trumpets sound...

I am in the arena for the final combat, the great joust. At the perimeter, the swarming and howling crowd of the people. On a platform shaded by a superb tent, the Count Palatine and other lords and ladies of the court; in their midst, Gertrude, whom I recognize by her white plume, but who cannot divine me in the black armor, the foreign blazon and the funereal emblem on my helm. By my side, the thirty ironclad cavaliers of my party; opposite, our thirty adversaries, visors lowered like ours, with their multicolored horse-coats, their gleaming weapons and their helmets decorated with heraldic beats.

I had chosen my adversary and placed myself facing him; it was Hartwig. He was wearing gray steel armor; at the crest of his helmet floated a golden yellow cloth decorated with blue serpents, Gertrude's colors.

I scarcely remember the combat. There was a furious initial impact, a second impact, and then an inextricable melee. Unsaddled, we drew our swords. The ardent battle remained silent. Our swords dropped, we drew daggers. Finally, we were fighting hand-to-hand, striking at the junctures. At the moment when Hartwig, bent backwards in my embrace, raised his arm for a great blow, my stiletto penetrated his neck through a breach in the gorgerin.

My adversary fell with a stifled cry. I put my knee on his breast and demanded that he surrender, but he made no reply. I lifted his visor; and I can still see, as if they were before me, that open mouth foaming with blood and those wide eyes that could no longer see me, but which, already fascinated by death and the gulf of eternity, had taken on something of the sublime and the sacred.

I shivered; all my anger drained away and I remember that in that rapid instant it was him that appeared to me to be the victor and me the vanquished. The thought of Gertrude returned me to my vengeance. I tore the yellow cloth from the crest. It was bloodstained. Through the tumult of the combat I climbed on to the platform without quitting my armor, with my visor lowered. Everyone moved side, struck by terror. Clinging to a wooden column, Gertrude watched me approach. I threw the scrap of bloodstained cloth in her face.

"Madame," I said, coldly, "here are your colors taken from your knight. You are responsible for his death. I return them to you; let whoever wishes wear them; henceforth I shall no longer dispute them with anyone. I am the one who avenges and does not pardon. Adieu."

She was livid with fear, but as I had said the last words in a tremulous voice a glimmer of triumph passed through her eyes. Frightened women fled; the counselors of the astonished prince ground their teeth and the guards brandished their halberds against me, but no one dared touch me, so much did my armed vengeance masked in black inspire fear. I was taken for some infernal administrator of justice, for a phantom of iron. I departed in the midst of general consternation. Only at a distance did a few voices cry: "Arrest that felon who insults a lady."

No one dared to follow me.

Night fell. I was galloping over a black plain striped with wan lights. I was fleeing the court, death, Gertrude and myself. My head was troubled. Sinister thoughts brushed me like bats.

I said to the bushes ranged among the edge of the road: "I have killed my rival!" and the bushes said, quivering: "What have you done for your brother-in-arms? He fell out there, strong and faithful; he died a hero. The gate of light is closing in the Orient."

I said to the owls that uttered their cry in the darkness: "I have avenged my honor!" and the owls replied: "Choo-hoo! Truly? What have you done for the angelic friend? What has become of the good fiancée? She is far away, and the pool of blood is filling a new abyss between you and her!"

I said to the clouds: "I have felled the Sphinx!" and the lightning replied: "The Sphinx is everywhere: in the flowing stream, in the dreaming lake, in the growing forest. The Sphinx is within you. You carry her harpoon in your flesh."

And I said to the mute earth, the implacable sky: "Where can I, the tracked and accursed, take refuge, where can I find shelter?" and the earth and the sky replied: "Go and hide in your last refuge, go and pray in the castle of your forefathers."

And I galloped and galloped over the black plain striped with wan lights.

VI. Rupertus's Ring

It was a sad return to Felseneck, to the maternal nest, the dilapidated sanctuary of my pure adolescence. The good chaplain and the honest Siegwart had died a long time ago. The watchman was asleep in his tower, the new servants no longer knew me. Trees were growing thick and straight at the foot of the keep; cracks split the walls. Grass was growing on the threshold of the doors; mildew covered the old tapestries. There was ruination, neglect and silence everywhere.

And my soul: what a ruin also! It had fallen to pieces. Oh, it certainly weighed upon me, the malediction of the Lord of the Seven Winds, and I was suffering for both the Staufens and the Felsenecks.

One day, I risked going into my mother's chapel. Such a thick layer of dust covered the painted windows that the saint and the knight seemed to be barely colored shadows. I gazed at Rupertus's ring and I bowed my head. A man requires three divine graces in order to accomplish is noble destiny: a Master who will show him the way; an Angel who will inspire him; and a Brother-in-Arms who will fight by his side. I had had those three graces, but I had forgotten and betrayed the Master, the Angel and the Brother for the vertigo of the Sphinx. Did those invisible guides still exist, or had they vanished too, vain shadows? My soul could scarcely perceive them, indecisive and veiled; they paled, ever fainter, ever more distant. Oh, the horrible moment when they would disappear completely! That menacing thought tortured me more than all the others.

When I emerged from the chapel I ordered that the windows be washed. Alas, one cannot wash the stains from one's soul like those on panted glass. And I could not cleanse mine of Gertrude's gazes, kisses and embraces. I was marked by them like burns. I hated her, but I was not free of her. What, then, was the invincible charm that linked me to the Sphinx? Did I not know, now, what the feminine monster was, the soulless beast with the powerful senses and the subtle brain? Why, in spite of everything, did she retain her hold over me? Why, having rejected her with so much energy, did I still feel enslaved by her? Was it because of the weakness of my senses? No: I had unmasked and challenged her in the grotto of spells. Was it out of cowardice? Nor that; I had chastised her in public...

No, the great culpable was my soul. It had lent itself to the envelopment of a magic that it could no longer break. It had allowed to germinate within itself a violent desire to penetrate the feminine enigma in all its metamorphoses, with the bitter desire to possess the entire sex in a single woman.

By day I succeeded in banishing her image or execrating it. At night she returned to haunt me in a thousand forms and a thousand attitudes. The memory of her adventure with Hartwig exasperated my folly.

"Who are you," I murmured, "who can feign all those souls?" Then I saw her smile as Enid, weep as Guinevere or threaten as Cleopatra. I surprised myself cursing her and appealing to her at the same moment. I burned under icy breaths. Subtle touches and sighs slid through the heavy air within the drapes. One might have thought it a bewitchment.

I succeeded in chasing away the obsession by reviving the noble and serene figure of Rupertus and the unique dream. By various paths, all the memories of my family brought me back to Berthe, the invisible but ever-present guest of the sanctuary of my soul. I affirmed resolutions by means of prayer and fasting. Day after day, Berthe returned to my memory purer and more intense.

One morning, I was asleep in my mother's great bed—an oak-wood bed with a baldaquin. With my eyes closed, I could perceive the whole room distinctly. A vague white form was standing between the window and me. On the height and breadth of its breast shone a great cross of fire; it did not have the appearance of a fabric but of a living fire that emerged from the very person. The white form extended its arms as if it were appealing to me. I made a great effort to get up, but in vain.

When I awoke, it had disappeared. In its place, the early morning sunlight was entered through the small panes of the windows. I experienced a frightful dolor at not having perceived its face. Could I doubt that it was Berthe? Was not the cross of fire on her breast the image of all her sacrifice and the unaccomplished dream of my entire life? Was it not the sign that she was about to ignite a similar cross of fire in my own breast, and set my heart ablaze for a supreme effort? By the holocaust of my evil life would I not be free, and myself, for the first time?

On a dark tempestuous night after a dismal autumn day of swirling leaves I found myself in my mother's bedroom, beside the bed with twisted columns. On my knees was a coffer taken from her cupboard, a coffer full of the tarnished jewels of ancestors. The wind was blowing as it had in the distant night of my adolescence when I had discovered the secret of my family in a conversation between my father and his neighbor. All day I had been thinking about the dispositions to make before my departure. Now I was looking toward the terrestrial future, the extreme struggle. I felt alone and mortally sad. Wilfried was no more and my true fiancée was nothing but a shadow of old, a dream, and impalpable spirit.

At that moment I heard the blast of the watchman's horn in the midst of the squall that was shaking the old walls of the castle. But I was so engrossed in my thoughts that I did not pay any attention to it and I continued my reverie.

Gradually, I felt myself becoming Konrad von Staufen again. I thought that it might have been the first night when I had taken my fiancée home on my return from the crusade…and my gaze could not quit a curtain that covered a door communicating via a staircase with the courtyard.

I shivered; the catch of the door had shifted; the curtain was raised. A woman in a gray mantle came though, her face hidden by a hooded cape. She stopped, her arms folded. Beside myself my hair standing on end, I gazed at the motionless and veiled shade, as if facing my personified destiny. Finally, I collapsed in my armchair; a cold sweat inundated me. The phantom had gained courage; it advanced a few paces and let its cape fall.

It was Gertrude.

At first I experienced a release and a relief. Gertrude brought back the terror of the unknown and the firm ground of reality. Bare-headed, her hair undone over her traveling costume, her arms still folded, she stood there, her eyes fixed on me. My initial surprise having passed, the blood that had flowed away from my heart violently rebounded toward my brain in a flood of anger.

"By what right are you here in my sanctuary?"

"Well, yes," she said without changing her posture, "you can't expel me from here. You've belonged to me since your childhood. I've conquered you and I want to keep you, Konrad."

"After your vile treason?"

"I didn't betray you, I avenged myself for your coldness, your insulting scorn. You mocked me with your indifference and your cruel abandonment. According to you I was no longer your wife when you bid me adieu at Hohenstein to run after your chimera. Then I drew that stupid weakling into my arms. I could have drawn a hundred others in order to twist the harpoon in your infidel and treacherous heart! But you came back to me, for you avenged yourself too, and your vengeance, which proved your love, bound you to me by a stronger tie.

"Do you know that you still love me, Konrad? Yes, you love me, and you will love me until your last sigh. You were able to overturn the cup with which I tried to enchant our ardent days and our appeased nights; you were able to scorn the magical voluptuousness desired by everyone; you were able to reject the tender Enid, the foolish Guinevere and the powerful Cleopatra, and all the women who agitate in my veins, but you could not stop desiring me! No, you cannot reject Gertrude, Gertrude…who is coming go you today…entirely!"

Her voice was vibrant, as bitter and sweet as her desire. Her arms opened; she extended her insinuating hands toward me. I recoiled several paces before the seductress, but she followed me, humbly suppliant—she, the proud and superb, Suddenly, she darted an ambiguous glance and whispered: "Do I not know that the

133

smoke of the blood shed by you is burning now in your blood like an inextinguishable flame?"

"Ah, wretched Sphinx," I said to her, "who makes even murder into sensuality, I hate you! Is this your new wedding? I hate you for having taken my courage; I hate you for the lies with which you have blinded me; and I curse you for the blood that you made me shed in a cowardly fashion!"

I had seized her by the wrists. She buckled under my effort.

"On the ground!" I cried.

She fell to her knees, half-reversed under an arm. I got a grip on myself, alarmed by my own violence. She remained as if vanquished for a few seconds; then, suddenly straightening up, still kneeling, but with her head high and her hands over her breast, she said:

"Well, so be it. Kill me, if you dare!"

I was nonplussed, she had dragged herself toward me; she had seized my knees with one hand, and with the other she indicated the location of the heart; breathlessly, she added: "You can strike Konrad, for I love you now!"

She was beautiful, with an infernal beauty, beautiful in crawling humility and imperious audacity, in her plea charged with challenge. The gulf of her eyes glittered.

"Wretch! Do you have a soul, then?" I murmured, afflicted by vertigo.

She uttered a cry of joy. Convulsively, in the blink of an eye, her fingers had taken possession of mine. With one bound, she was sitting on my knees. I felt her burning mouth simultaneously on my hair, my eyes and my lips, still chilled by terror.

"Yes, now I have one!" she clamored.

And she drank my breath avidly. Under her profound inhalation, I had the sentiment that she was drawing off half of my life. I lost all my strength, as if a monstrous serpent were holding me in its coils. She tried to drag me toward the bed, where a little lamp was shining. Attached to the ceiling of the baldaquin, it illuminated the curtains gently with its familial light. In that nimbus Gertrude spread her corrupting magic. I was about to yield, but the image of my mother passed before my eyes.

I tore myself away violently.

"No! No!" I stammered. "Today, I need to be alone; I'll leave you..."

And I fled abruptly, abandoning my mother's bed to her. I went out without looking back. But at the moment when I closed the door I heard Gertrude's languid voice sigh a farewell: "Until tomorrow!"

And that terrible "Until tomorrow!" pursued me in the darkness of the spiral stairway.

That night, I went into the forest. I stopped from time to time and, feeling myself totter. I leaned on fir-trees streaming with rain, curbed by the storm, and I said to myself that if the Sphinx had a soul I would be doomed. *Has she not stolen half of mine already? Can she attract the other half with that? She is installed now in my stronghold; is she going to install herself in my heart? What should I resolve? What can I do?*

The crowns of the tall firs were colliding with one another in the darkness. Sometimes, one of them cracked, broken by the tempest. I was marching without seeing anything, without hearing anything. Oh, the kisses of the Sphinx, more terrible than the hurricane!

The next day, Gertrude came to find me in the great hall. She approached me with the calm and the authority of a chatelaine. She extended her hand to me so graciously that I could not refuse her mine. It was her who seemed to be forgiving me. A dull anger rumbled within me. I felt ready to do something extraordinary, but I did not know what.

She divined my hidden revolt but believed herself to be sure of her victory. Had she not, if not vanquished me, at least check-mated me the previous evening? She was one of those women whose smile disarms and whose gaze commands. She became more joyful and more expansive because I was more somber and more enclosed.

"Show me the castle—*our* castle," she said, smiling.

I stood up; she took my arm and I obeyed.

I explained the history of my ancestors to her before their armor suspended from the pillars of the hall.

"What fêtes we shall give here!" she said. "Felseneck will flourish again with all the wealth of Hohenstein."

She wanted to go up to the top of the keep, and having reached the terrace she cried: "How beautiful it is! How wild it is! These forests, these villages and the rich plain! And all this is ours! Will you love me more as the huntress of Felseneck than as the siren of Hohenstein? I'll make myself a huntress…and the nixies of the lakes, tell me, shall we awaken them? Will they want to visit us in the silence of the nights, when I reign alone?"

Her supple hand slid along my arm; her hair brushed my cheek. I made no reply, but I sensed her will take possession of all the trees of my domain and all the fibers of my body. I was similar to a living tree myself, labored by a saw and perforated by a drill. Something in the depths of my self would have liked to precipitate her from the tower, and yet my desire devoured her with caresses, while I remained as mute and cold as marble. We descended in silence to the courtyard of the castle. She leaned toward my ear and whispered: "Come into your mother's bedroom!"

The certainty of the triumph was legible in the depths of her eyes. I believed myself doomed, when I sudden idea opened an escape route to me like a ray of light.

"This," I said, "is my mother's chapel. Would you like to come in with me?"

"Why not?" she replied, nonchalantly.

We went in. The virgin of the window and the knight of the terrible forest were fulgurant again in their original splendor. They evoked the sovereign thoughts of my life. Under their gaze I steeped myself again in a pure atmosphere. I invoked Rupertus, Berthe and the God of sacred hours. I spoke to them; they replied to me. I had rediscovered my complete consciousness and my full will.

"It's cold in this tomb; let's get out!" Gertrude said to me, abruptly, sensing an unknown and hostile influence.

"No, on the contrary, let's stay," I said, firmly, holding her by the arm. "At Hohenstein, didn't you take me into the grotto of the lake, your sanctuary? This is mine, and if you want to be the chatelaine of Felseneck, it's necessary that you know it. Look at that sarcophagus, where a marble woman with joined hands is asleep, her faithful greyhound curled up at her feet. It's my mother's. I'm the son of her amour and her dolor. She gave birth to me for a severe and mysterious destiny.

"Look at the unknown Saint, the virgin in stained glass with the flamboyant heart. I came to adore her in my childhood. She is the annunciatrix of the invisible fiancée. Look at that knight emerging from the terrible forest in order to launch himself into the battle. That's me, that's Konrad von Staufen, the crusader, resuscitated in Konrad de Felseneck and destined to redeem the malediction that weighs upon my race, to show my brethren the way of truth...

"That's the divine destiny that I have chosen. And it's you, perverse Sphinx, heart of a vampire in the body of a siren, who wants to turn me away from it. Because you have no soul, you have come to drink mine, all the way to my sanctuary. You want to glorify yourself with my defeat and live on my death. But that soul you shall not have; I shall unmask your void and you shall only live here defeated and devoid of strength."

All her hatred of a crushed snake seemed to spring from her eyes and her mouth, in a jet of venom.

"Miserable coward!" she said. "Ingrate and fool! Yes, I scorn men for their pride and their weakness. They melt like snow in my hands. But you, whom I believed to be strong and generous, on whom I lavished all the arcana of my magic, whom I would have made the king of the earth, you dare to insult me, like one of your feeble mistresses? Be accused! I loved you. Now I hate you; woe betide you! My power is a match for yours, and you will perish entirely!"

I folded my arms and remained impassive. Seeing me armored against her this time, she clutched the edge of the sculpted wooden bench as if she wanted to rip it from the ground.

"Who, then." she said, "gives you your power?"

"You don't believe in other powers than your own. Do you see this ring? It's the ring of my betrothal with the invisible angel. So long as I wear it on my finger, you can do nothing against me. By virtue of it I command you, by means of it I banish you from my sanctuary. You will not reenter my mother's chamber and you will depart tomorrow. Pursue your destiny; but take care, no longer put yourself in my path. You can do nothing against this force.

Her troubled gaze went from my eyes at the ring, and from the ring to my eyes. She sniggered and said: "Oh, so that's your secret? You have a invisible fiancée? Love her, then! I don't care about that and I don't fear her. But in your turn, take care. For having said that to me, you'll suffer for the rest of your life!"

She went out with a grim gesture and an oblique glance, full of sly mockery.

Shut away all day, I surrounded myself with my dear memories, like a defensive wall. Retired to another wing of the castle, Gertrude did not reappear before my eyes. She had ordered her servants to be ready to leave the next day.

Night fell, and I went to sleep peacefully in my mother's bed, under the heavy oak baldaquin, which also seemed an ancestral chapel. During my slumber, sumptuous perfumes enveloped me with thick veils. Drawn by them, I descended toward a marshy terrain. A dying light trailed over pale willows and black rushes. A large number of women, wretchedly dressed, were walking on the edge of the troubled water. I recognized some of them. They all seemed sad.

"We are your sins," they said. "We are your accomplices. Will you not come to deliver us?"

I replied to each one: "Yes, I will come."

Finally, I perceived Gertrude behind a bush, who was gazing at me, her arms folded, with her menacing expression. She seemed to be saying: "But you did not have pity for me!"

The landscape and the women faded away. An enervating fluid ran through my brain and diluted my will. In the effort I made to shake it off, I opened my eyes.

The little lamp above me had just gone out—under what unexpected breath or malevolent finger? The moon was shining through the window panes. A kneeling woman was leaning against my bed. I could only see her hair scattered over her shoulders. Raising myself up partly on the edge of my bed I remained motionless, frozen with terror before that white form, softly bathed and blue-tinted by moonlight.

Finally, I found the strength to say: "Who's there?"

"Your servant, your slave," replied the woman, still motionless, in a low voice.

I had recognized Gertrude.

Hoisting herself up a little toward my face, she stammered: "Listen, Konrad, I'm leaving at daybreak; I'm leaving, and whatever you do, you'll never see me again. Just now I watched you sleeping and I dreamed that I was yours once more...once more...and then, never again!"

"No! Go away; get out!"

"Adieu, then," she said.

And she collapsed dolorously.

Her humble and defeated attitude made her resemble a repentant and passionately submissive Magdalen. Her imperious beauty had dissolved in a char of tender voluptuousness. She seemed to be on the point of fainting, and the illusion of a soul agonizing in the disorder if that beautiful body lent her a supreme seduction.

"Gertrude!" A surge of deadly pity and cowardly compassion wrung that cry from me.

She had seized my extended hand. Almost immediately, I felt perfumed hair on my face, a fiery mouth on my mouth. All thought quit me. Vanquished prey, I abandoned myself to the bitter embrace of the Sphinx, to her lips, which drank my soul with a vampiric thirst.

What a lugubrious awakening there was at the dawn of that frenzied night! It was like those of my childhood when I said to myself: "Who am I? How was I born? From what void have I emerged?" The curtains of the bed were drawn, but broad daylight filtered through a large gap in the penumbra of the alcove. First I perceived the night-light that was hanging sadly from the baldaquin, like a dead lamp over a tomb. A torpor numbed me; no memory echoed in the empty darkness of my brain. But now they all surged forth at once before a terrible presence!

Lying beside me, propped up on her elbow, a woman was gazing at me with eyes as cruel and as profound as gulfs. It was really Gertrude, but Gertrude reinforced in her highest power and as if hardened, the terrible Sphinx of my dream, the marble Sphinx! Yes, marble! With the superb immodesty and the serene pride of statues, she presented her two breasts like white shields, their rosy tips changed by victory into dots of bloody crimson.

Then it seemed to me that that woman, who had just drunk all the sighs and all the flames of my life, was about to crush me in her arms of stone. I could neither speak nor move; I considered her with anguish. And she

141

too remained motionless, her head supported by her hand...

Suddenly, that anguish turned to fear; on that hand, knotted in the gold of her hair, I had seen the ring with the amethyst stone shining! It was in order to steal the sacred object from me while I slept that she had seduced and tamed me, in spite of myself. And now it was glittering n the finger of the Sphinx, the ring of my mystical betrothal, the guardian of my power, the star of salvation!

I raised myself up on my elbow and I said: "By what right to you wear that ring?"

She replied to me with her smile and her enigmatic voice, in which there was irony, languor and triumph.

"Did you not cry to me last night, three times, in the midst of unusual transports, "I love you!" Your dreams have deceived you, my friend. It is me who was the Fiancée, and now I am the Wife. The ring belongs to me. Does not the wife have the right to wear the sign of marriage?

While she was speaking I had blushed with shame and paled with anger, but I remained mute. Had the thief of the ring also stolen my faith in the invisible fiancée, which was my safeguard? I did not have the strength to snatch her trophy from her. She was right, the Sphinx: she had spoken the frightful truth. It was not only my senses that had failed in that fatal night; my soul had foundered in giving itself to the Enemy. I slid out of the alcove like a malefactor, more frightened of myself than of Gertrude. Then I went out silently, head bowed.

And I remember spending that day wandering in the woods like a wild beast. I walked without seeing anything. I was like a man fallen into a gulf with no issue.

From my dark well, the sky was no longer anything but a wan mouth of the abyss. Very high, between two rocks, the beautiful, horrible Sphinx still appeared to me, her breasts bare, her claws out and her smiling head leaning over the depth of my fall.

I plunged into thickets, I tore myself on thorns, I went up the bed of torrents on large stones. Nothing helped; my thoughts went on, descending in a spiral all the steps of my Hell. Then a certainty more frightful more frightful than all the others took possession of me; not only had I lost my celestial guardian forever, but I no longer believed in her...

Rupertus, Berthe, the dream in the ruin, all that was nothing but smoke, illusion and lies; and the woman of flesh, the sovereign and indomitable Sphinx, reigned alone over my brain.

There is something more terrible for a man than his fall itself, which is no longer to believe in his dream. To doubt oneself is only a failing, but to doubt the Truth is the death of the soul. With faith, one can climb out of any abyss, without it, one falls back from every summit; without it, reason and will are only blind hands and feet. Faith is Amour in action; it is happiness and it is heaven. Doubt is the utmost depths of dolor, the arcana of Hell.

I had reached that black doubt...the heart of darkness. Oh, the ring, to recapture the ring! But that was impossible.

The mere thought of seeing Gertrude again and being subject again to the magic of her gaze and the delights of her imperious embrace made me shiver from head to toe. What would become of me? I had lost my guide, thrown my lamp into the abyss.

Already the dusk was filtering lamentably though the bushy forest. The setting sun was descending like a red globe through the tall fir trees, setting ablaze the bases of the tightly-packed trunks, illuminating dying furnaces in the thickness of the wood. Finally, everything was extinguished. Only a cloud in the ocean of the sky still displayed its blazing band behind the somber firwood. Oh, that island of fire floating in the azure, that blessed isle, as if bleeding over my accursed darkness! It was carrying my protective angels away: Rupertus, Berthe and Wilfried; strength, the dream and hope. I saw it pale, and the night was black.

Fear gripped me. I had no other shelter than my castle, which had become the lair of the Sphinx. It was necessary to lend myself to one last struggle with the monster, to be devoured or to recover the ring. How? I did not know. I trembled involuntarily, but an obscure need for deliverance led me through the darkness to the postern without my having sought my path or remarked my route.

I entered my home with a furtive tread, like a thief. I turned round continually to see whether anyone had seen me. I had never experienced an anguish like the one I felt as I climbed the stairway that led from the floor below to my mother's bedroom, inhabited by Gertrude.

I expected to find her up and about, and prepared myself to confront her gaze and her voice. I was very surprised to see her in bed and asleep, by the light of the little lamp. Her slumber frightened me, like a tortuous cavern with tenebrous counsel.

She was sinisterly beautiful in her nocturnal garment, her cheek resting on her folded arm, with a evil crease at the corner of her mouth, her hand closed in a gesture of possession that does not release its prey, and, shining on the ring-finger, Rupertus's ring. The mild amethyst had the gaze of a martyrized angel. That sight had the effect on me of a dagger thrust; convulsively, I gripped the hilt of the sharply-pointed stiletto that I wore n my belt.

The thought of murder had just entered into me, sharp and suffocating. What! Strike a sleeping woman? That was infamous and cowardly. No, the blade did not want to come out of the sheath; no, I could not.

She sighed...

I thought she was about to open her eyes, but her sleep became more profound. Her face took on a sly expression. She began to speak in her hoarse voice, which was her demonic voice:

"Konrad...the fiancée is dead...it's me who has killed her...and now your soul belongs to me! With the blood of your heart...I shall revive...yes, revive...finally live again!"

I was frozen with horror, and my heart stopped for several seconds. But at the same time, I had a strange perception. It seemed to me that I saw, under the whiteness of the breast, her heart contracting and palpitating, gorged on lust and death, her heart of a Sphinx, from which the blood emerged red with desire and returned blue with treason...

Then I struck, accurately, with all the strength of my arm, and the knife plunged in to the hilt. She sat up as if moved by a spring, with the shrill cry of a wild beast, such as has never been heard, clenched her hands momentarily upon my arm and looked at me with her abyssal eyes, immeasurably open—and then fell back, a heavy mass, with a hiccup.

I recall that in the following minutes, when I gazed at her, bewildered by my sudden action and the hideous spectacle of the accomplished murder, I had no remorse. I only experienced a profound amazement at the sight of those empty eyes, that face fixed in the ultimate fear, and all that womanly magic, capsized in a warm cadaver. The indelible image was engraved in my eyes. Suddenly, it frightened me. Swiftly, I withdrew Rupertus's ring from her inert hand, and I fled.

That same night I quit the paternal castle, never to see it again.

VIII. The Angel

And I have been to the crusade. I have fought on the Danube frontier; I have seen the Crescent flee. I entered Belgrade with the victors, but I did not feel the divine kiss of Victory and the great Liberator—Death—has fled me.

Afterwards, I visited the Holy Land as a pilgrim. In the midst of my companions, peasants, warriors or monks, I remained the wanderer, the solitary, the exile. I became the nameless knight, the stranger who passes by and whom no one salutes.

And everywhere, on the dusty roads, in the cut-throat mountains where the ambush lies in wait; by night under the tent erected on the black plains in which bivouac fires burns; on the battlefields where the cries of the wounded mingle with the whinnying of horses; in the decorated palaces of princes as in fetid leprosaria; and even under the vaults of this peaceful convent where the brothers of Saint Benedict have received me—everywhere—the image of the Sphinx has followed me; everywhere I have dreamed her broken gaze, the horror of her bloodied beautiful body, the agony of her tresses scattered in a crimson pool...

You have pursued me with your voluptuous hatred and your implacable amour, O Sphinx! Your obsessive image has enabled me to know a new torture, that of impure desires stimulated by burning remorse...and death had rendered you invulnerable. I could not stab you again while you floated over the darkness of my bed. Yes you have possessed me, you have burned me, even in the depths of sanctuaries!

147

And all that is still nothing. The veritable punishment is that I have tried in vain to recall Berthe. I no longer heard the voice of the Angel in the flame of beautiful sunsets; no luminous dram haunted any longer my early morning slumber. In spite of my penitence, I was abandoned, accursed.

One day, in Syria, before a bare cloister, under the devouring sun, near the yellow desert, the profound Voice, the Voice of Silence spoke to me and said:

"To kill is not to vanquish, it changes the visible adversary into an invisible and ever-present enemy. The only certain victory is renunciation followed by combat. You killed the Sphinx in order to recover the ring. Who knows whether it was not necessary for you to be reborn in order to find the true crusade and fight the triumphant fight? Expiate, Konrad von Staufen; expiate, Konrad von Felseneck, When the Sphinx who lives through you has rendered the last sigh, then, palm in hand and myrtle on the forehead, the glorious fiancée will return."

I have become a monk, and now I am at the end of my strength, worn away by my fatigue, aged by my thoughts. The pale Sphinx sometimes prowls around me still. She has become sad and timid. Now I feel pity for her; I weep for her and I pray for her deliverance. To weep is to forgive, and to forgive is to vanquish. She weeps too; she weeps as she draws away, insinuating and redoubtable.

The hours drag. I am afraid of red roses; they remind me of Gertrude's breasts and the blood that sprang forth under my hand. I am afraid of white roses; they remind me of the myrtle flowers in Berthe's hair and the ecstasy of the mystical betrothal. This morning, for the first time, I dared to pick a white rose in the garden of the cloister. How that intoxicated me! What a supernatural joy ran through my heart, what a harmony with the essence of all beings! Was it the mouth of my dead dream that posed on my forehead? Was it a presentiment of the great final peace?

More months passed. This evening, I looked for a long time at the amethyst on my finger. It emitted a pale, gentle spark. It is tarnished; now it only lights up feebly. In spite of everything, I've kept your ring, Rupertus. There are days that devour all the years of our lives because they contain Eternity, like the one when I encountered you, Master whom I scarcely glimpsed, more beloved than all men, you who bore in your old man's eyes a flame move vivid than the flame that one sees in twenty-year-old eyes. What has become of you, you who were the only one able to read the depths of my soul? Do you reside on one of the stars that served you as emblems to figure the laws that register our destinies? Or are you no longer anything but a volatile substance, a quintessence inaccessible in the universe?

Last night I dreamed that I found myself on a pointed rock in the middle of a white fog, and behind that mist someone was singing in an unknown language. But the voice itself resembled the sighs that the wind extracts from an Aeolian harp suspended among ruins: subtle, shrill and palpitating with celestial passion...

Another voice, more profound, which emerged from somewhere nearby, said to me:

"This fog is what remains of your terrestrial passions, which prevents you from discovering the Truth. Thus far, you have only seen the vulgar form that veils the spirit. Soon you will see the Light that the soul manifests in the boldness and the splendor of its purity."

"What is that song" I asked.

"Do you remember the sad brunette with the violet eyes weaving myrtles in her dark tresses? Her gaze is a gaze of eternity, her kiss a kiss of victory..."

What silence! The little bell of the convent is ringing for vespers. Tonight, the nightingale died in its cage outside the prior's cell. That is why everything has fallen silent. The bird is asleep and I too am going to sleep; my blood is only beating feebly in my veins now; life is evaporating from my brain like drops of dew in the morning sun...

Oh that voice of the Aeolian harp, which is traversing infinite space...if only I could still hear it!

The Sphinx is dying...is that the Angel who is coming?

TINTORETTO'S PUPIL

I

Tintoretto was walking one evening on the Quay of Slaves. He hardly ever quit his work, but sometime forgot himself on that populous shore, where the costumes and types of the entire Orient pullulated in those days in a picturesque mélange.

The evening was warm, the sky clear. Innumerable moored boats aligned their prows along the quay. On the flagstones the variegated population of the port swarmed pell-mell. Here Turks were smoking in a circle, there Illyrian coasters with the profiles of pirates were supping on the decks of their boats. A well-nourished Franciscan was begging alongside a thin Jewish money-changer who was clinking the gold on his table. Further away, the sailors of the arsenal were fighting with Egyptian acrobats. Even further away gentlemen were bargaining with an Armenian for semi-naked Georgian slaves who were hiding behind bales of merchandise. Here and there, in open-air cooking-pots, the large red polyps that the people of Venice call *frutti di mare* were roasting. Mountains of melons rolled on the ground; girandoles were beginning to blaze, and children danced around.

The master traversed the groups at a rapid pace, more alone in that crowd than in his studio. In the vanity of the arsenal he stopped dead. A Turkish galiot had dropped anchor a short distance away. Two richly-

151

dressed young lords were arguing win loud voices with a small sun-tanned man with a hooked nose and large drooping eyelids.

"This child is mine," said one of the gentlemen, who was wearing a red toga and a white silk toque co-quettishly poised on his long blond hair. "He's mine, I tell you, because you sold him to me a little while ago for twenty golden ducats."

"Excuse me, Signor," the merchant jabbered. in a baroque Italian. "Sold, no; promised, yes, on condition that no one offered me more during the day."

"The devil whispered that in my ear," said the other gentleman, a superb brown-haired fellow in a black velvet mantle embroidered with gold. "I was passing at the time, and without having heard anything, I saw the child and offered thirty ducats for him."

"And honorably, he belongs to Your Excellency," said the merchant.

"Not so fast," said the other. "If it's an auction, I'm in. I offer forty ducats."

"Well then, fifty!"

"Continue, messires, continue," said the merchant. "I'm in no hurry."

During the conversation, Tintoretto had approached the merchant and whispered in his ear: "Is it a young woman that these young fools are disputing?"

"No, it's a young Greek twelve years old. Each of the two is determined to take him for a page. Refrain from interrupting; they're going strong."

"And where is the child?"

"Over there, on the edge of the quay."

Tintoretto took a few steps toward the bank. A boy was sitting on the flagstones, leaning his back against a crate, his legs dangling over the water. A velvet jacket embroidered with gold added to his present misery the memory of some past splendor; but the child did not seem unhappy. He was drawing something with a piece of charcoal on a wooden board, with an absorbed expression.

"What are you doing there, my friend?" asked Tintoretto.

The child raised a challenging gaze to the stranger and continued drawing without saying anything.

"You've learned to draw?"

No response.

"It's a woman's head that you're making there. Is it someone you've seen?"

The child got up, in an irritated manner, but, suddenly reassured by the unknown man's benevolent gaze, he handed him the board, exclaiming: "It's my mother!"

His large dark eyes flashed, and a beautiful smile gilded his pale face. The painter examined the profile. It was delicately drawn; it resembled the child's. The suave line of the forehead was recognizable, the proud gaze, and the fine arch of the eyebrow.

"You've done that from memory?

"I draw my mother every evening. If I had colors I'd make her even more beautiful."

"Where are you from?"

"Cyprus."

"And your mother is still there?"

"My mother died two years ago. Then the pirates took me and sold me to that man. He told me that he would enable me to see Venice, an island more beautiful than ours. Here we are, but there are no mountains."

The little Cypriot designated with a scornful gesture the flat strip of the Lido, already drowned in the gray of dusk. Suddenly, however, he let his extended arm drop, and as if the sharp sensation of the eternal separation suddenly penetrated his childish consciousness, he lowered his eyes full of tears, and added, in a low voice: "And then…my mother is no longer there!"

Tintoretto was not easily moved; he had suffered and struggled to much himself to feel facile compassionate for others; but at the sight of that poor human plant uprooted from his native soil, in whom the flower of the beautiful was only asking to blossom, he sensed his artistic brain seething and his human heart beating faster. An idea crossed his mind.

"What is your name?" he said to the child.

"Dimitri."

"Well, Dimitri, which would you prefer: to be the domestic of one of those fine lords over there, who want to buy you, or to be my pupil. They're rich, and I'm poor, but if you wish, I'll teach you to paint."

"Signor," said the radiant child, "I want to go with you."

"Good. Wait for me."

Tintoretto rejoined the group of buyers. The bidding had risen to a hundred ducats, and the two gentlemen still had not given in.

"By the body of Bacchus," said one, "let me have the child, or my friendship for you is ended."

"By the blood of Diana," replied the other, "stop disputing him with me, or I'll become your enemy."

"Remember, Loredani, that I'm protected by the Duke of Ferrara!"

"Remember, Barbarello, that I'm the cousin of the Doge of Venice!"

"In truth," said Tintoretto, interposing himself between them, "it's a pleasure to see youth in dispute and good blood rising to the heads of dashing cavaliers, but may it please God, sires, that two lords of your merit don't fall out over a child. The Republic of Venice would suffer, and I, the humblest of its citizens, would be sorry. If one of you takes that little Greek away, the other will never forgive him. Instead of cutting one another's throats for him, yield him to me. I'll buy him."

"Well, I prefer that," said the Venetian.

"Me too," said the Ferraran.

"Then it's settled, my lords. Thank you very much; you're doing a good deed."

"And you! You've just conserved intact the amity between the joyful Ludovic Loredani and the no less insouciant Maffeo Barbarello, both of them being part of the blessed brotherhood of the blue trousers, the members of which are called the Flourishing and the Immortals. To whom do we owe the joy of our reconciliation? It must at least be to a senator."

"You're mistaken, Signor Loredani. I'm only a poor painter, named Jacopo Robusti."[7]

"What! You're Tintoretto?"

"Nothing but that, dear Immortal, and no more: a man who works eighteen hours a day and makes paintings for nothing, to the despair of all his peers. Design of Michelangelo and colors of Titian; for thirty years that has been the sign on my shop, and I won't change it."

"By Jupiter and by the Madonna, it has rendered you famous throughout Italy, and I'm a great fool not to have recognized you. Permit me, Robusti, to shake the hand of the foremost master in Venice. And since the child pleases you, permit us, Barbarello and me, to give

---

[7] Like "Tintoretto," Jacopo Robusti was also a nickname, but his baptismal name, Jacopo Comin, was not discovered until 2007.

him to you; for we don't want you to spent a ducat on the little fellow."

"Then you'd take away from me the joy I have in giving him liberty. I am too thankful to you, my lords, for the courtesy you have had in yielding them to me."

"What about my hundred ducats?" cried the merchant.

"Here they are," said Tintoretto, giving the Turk a purse full of gold. "Count them; you'll see that not one is missing."

"Poor fellow; you'll ruin yourself!" said Loredani.

"Not in the least. The Brotherhood of Saint-Roch gives me that sum for every painting I finish on the walls of its convent. I completed one yesterday; I'll commence another tomorrow."

"And what will you do with that child?"

"Tel me first what you would have done with him yourself," said Robusti. And his lip took on a sardonic curl. It was his fashion of smiling.

"I would have made him a guitar player," said Barbarello.

"And me a Hellenist," said Loredani.

"And I want to make a painter of him," said Tintoretto, resolutely. "Come back to my studio in five years and you'll have news of him. My lords, it's late, I render you my homage."

So saying, Master Jacopo returned to the bank. Dimitri was sitting sadly on the flagstones, still gazing at the lagoon. That gaze seemed to be searching the sea beyond the Lido. The dusk had thrown a veil of melancholy over his face. Was he thinking about his island?

"It's done," said the painter, in a brusque tone. "You're coming with me."

Dimitri leapt with joy and grasped his liberator's hand with an expression that said more than all thanks. The man and the child disappeared into the crowd.

"A great madman, that Tintoretto," said Barbarello, throwing his cloak back over his shoulder.

"But a fine painter," replied Loredani, adjusting the clasp of his beret.

"And a fine man," added the merchant, clinking in his hand the sequins that he had just counted.

II

That happened in the year 1566. Tintoretto was then fifty-four years old,[8] and his vogue was beginning to match that of old Titian, who was seventy-nine. The abandoned child had reminded the master of a dolorous episode in his youth. It is well-known that Titian, divining the genius of Tintoretto from a few sketches and scenting a dangerous rival, had him expelled from his studio. On seeing Dimitri, Tintoretto had thought: *I will do for that child what Titian should have done for me*. He adopted him, in spite of his wife and his two sons, Marco and Domenico, who had no talent for painting.

In fact, he was not mistaken about Dimitri's natural dispositions; his lively intelligence was combined with an ardent passion for art. Soon, the child was initiated into all the secrets of the métier. After two years, the master could no longer do without the pupil.

Tintoretto's wife, seeing the preference that her husband had for the boy she called "the foundling," burst into bitter tears. Robusti made her shut up by lodging his adoptive son with his neighbor, the gondolier Gianni; but Dimitri remained no less the cherished child of his soul. The people, who have a sure intuition and an instinctive understanding of great affections, were not mistaken about that. When the people of the quarter perceived the handsome adolescent in the distance, who did not seem to see anyone but whose beauty attracted all

---

[8] Tintoretto is now thought to have been born in 1518, so he would have been forty-eight in 1566

gazes, they cried: "*Ecco il figliuolo d'anima del Tinto-retto!*"[9]

Six years went by. It was 1571, a date celebrated in the annals of Venice by the victory of Lepanto.[10] Tintoretto, having got up early, was working, as usual, in his studio, a vast and high room that had once been the refectory of a convent. Daylight entered it through a large window veiled by a white blind. Thus filtered, the light allowed a mysterious penumbra to float in the depths of the room, but the strange objects that populated it stood out in the gloom with the powerful relief of chiaroscuro.

Four colossal figures were lying in the corners of the enormous studio and appeared to be the divinities of the lace. They were Michelangelo's Dawn, Dusk, Night and Day, reproduced in plaster by Daniel Volterra. An infinity of sketches in oil, drawings in charcoal, and water-colors covered the walls. On a table, in a multicolored scintillation, there was a host of velvet doublets, bronzes, silver cups and damascenes armor; on the floor, a pell-mell of plaster arms, hands, torsos and human masks seemed to be awaiting animation by some god; wax figurines suspended from the ceiling by invisible wires floated in a luminous dust beneath the somber beams, like errant spirits.

---

[9] Author's note: "The people of Venice made use of that poetic expression in those days to designate children adopted by charity."

[10] At the naval battle of Lepanto on 7 October 1571 a Christian fleet led by ships of the Venetian Republic and the Spanish Empire defeated the fleet of the Ottoman Turks, putting an end to the expansion of the Ottoman Empire through the Mediterranean.

As for the master, he was standing on a scaffold, half way up a fifty-foot canvas that collided with the ceiling. He was painting, with a kind of fury, his Last Judgment, for the Church of Santa Maria dell'Orto. The lower half of the canvas was finished; the upper, prepared with gypsum and roughly sketched in charcoal, was still awaiting the brush in order to emerge from the void. Robusti was painting vigorously with broad brushstrokes. Two ravishing naked young women were in the process of blossoming beneath his hand. Lifted up by the wind of the resurrection, smiling as on the first day of life, they were floating, half-enlaced, over the somber chaos, and seemed to be hesitating half way between Hell and Paradise.

"Dimitri!" cried Tintoretto. "Venetian white, cochineal red and ultramarine blue! Are you asleep? My palette is empty!"

And Dimitri crushed his colors on the marble and climbed on to the platform. The formidable brush of the master was throwing the paint in masses on to the canvas when someone knocked on the door. On opening a small window he saw two gentlemen in the street clad in velvet and silk.

"What do you want?" he said. "I don't have time to waste."

"I'm Ludovico Loredani," said one of them, "and I've come on behalf of the Doge to commission you to paint the battle of Lepanto."

"That's different," said Robusti, opening the door gallantly. "My brushes are at the service of the Republic."

Loredani entered with his friend Maffeo Barbarello, glad to profit from the opportunity to see the studio into which Tintoretto, jealous of his methods, only allowed a few intimate friends to penetrate. They started chatting. Maffeo's eyes fell upon Dimitri, who was observing the visitors from the depths of his corner. He saw the distinguished appearance of the young man of eighteen years. His long dark fair, curly and parted in the middle of the forehead in the "Nazarene manner," as it was known in the Orient, gave him a particular grace. His exquisitely suave head moved with ease over broad shoulders; his delicate features floated between the type of Eros and that of Psyche,

"Master," said Maffeo, surprised by the beauty of that face, "where does that child come from?"

"What! You don't recognize him? It's the little Greek that you were disputing with Signor Loredani five or six years ago on the Quay of Slaves."

"And you took him from us, that's right. It would have been better, dear master, to leave him to us. He would have been a ravishing page; but a painter, him? He's too pretty for that."

Dimitri, who had keen ears, shivered. He seized a piece of paper at random and started dashing off a sketch with a feverish pencil. Maffeo, who did not lose sight of him while continuing the conversation, perceived that Dimitri was gazing at him with ardent eyes while he worked. After a few minutes he marched straight up to the pupil and snatched the piece of paper away from him.

"See the little ingrate," he said to Loredani, hand over the drawing. "He's just made my caricature."

"Charming," said Loredani. "With those horns you give the impression of a devil on the lookout for a passing soul. The resemblance is striking, although charged. When you win while gambling or watch a woman passing by, you have that expression."

"Including the coiffure?" asked Maffeo, laughing curtly. "Thank you very much. My compliments, Master; you've won your bet. The boy has talent, and he's of your school; anyone who brushes him gets stung!"

"Excuse him, Signor; he's a child," said Robusti, incapable of hiding his joy.

The two gentlemen took their leave of Tintoretto. In the doorway, Maffeo turned to the apprentice with a protective smile and threw at him: "No hard feelings, Dimitri. I forgive you for your talent. You'll soon come to make my portrait in oils."

When Robusti was alone with Dimitri he picked up the sketch and then threw it into a corner. "Not bad for a joke, but it's daubing. When will you do something serious?"

Two large tears filled the pupil's eyes and trickled down his cheeks. "Master! I work day and night, and never yet have you said to me: 'That's good!' When will I be a painter, then?"

"A painter? A painter!" muttered Tintoretto, with a grim and surly expression. "Do you know what that means: a painter? Do you suspect it, by chance? Beautiful colors can be bought in the shops of the Rialto, but design is only obtained from the jewel-case of genius. Painting is like the sea; the more one sails on it the rougher it becomes. You're scarcely able to copy nature; will you be capable of creating beauty? Nature only gives you a sketch; only genius can finish it. It's not only a matter of working, it's a matter of suffering, of struggling, and above all of willing!

"I, Robusti, such as you see me, daubed like you from the age of four, like the true son of a dyer that I was. But do you want to know how I became Tintoretto? Listen! Everyone covered me with shame, Titian and the rest. I only had one joy, a woman that I loved madly, a daughter of the Frioul archipelago, a superb blonde with the eyes of a magicienne. She betrayed me; I wanted to kill her, and then kill myself. But I changed my mind and went home. I burned the portrait I'd made of her, took a fresh canvas and made another. I painted her in her deceptive beauty, in her perfidious charm, such as I had seen her in another's arms. Oh, that evening I burned with all the flames of amour and jealousy; I loved her more than ever and I painted her with all the blood of my heart. I worked for a part of the night by the light of that lantern. Finally, felled by fatigue, I rolled into bed. In the morning I got up and I looked at my canvas and I felt that I was a master! Well, my child, I'm waiting for the day when you fall in love. What you do then will give me your measure. But if you tremble before the woman, woe betide you; you won't be a painter."

Robusti had spoken animatedly. With an abrupt gesture he picked up his palette and climbed the scaffold again. Dimitri resumed crushing lapis lazuli in a pensive manner. Tintoretto's words seemed very strange to him, and he searched in his mind, but in vain, for the means of becoming a master.

III

A few days later, all the bells in Venice rang. The doge, aboard the *Bucentaur* with the whole Senate, went to receive the victorious general, Sebastiano Veniero, at the Lido. Dmitri set forth, wandering through the city at random. After many detours he reached the extremity of the Grand Canal, which serves today as a customs post. There, a prodigious sight made him marvel.

The *Bucentaur*, which had brought the Senate and the general from the Lido, had stopped some distance from the ducal palace. Thousands of boats were ringing the ship, like seagulls around a monstrous golden phoenix.

Closer at hand there was a multicolored shimmer of velvet, silk and ermine. The Grand Canal disappeared under an infinite number of luxury gondolas, boats large and small. Flag-decked skiffs passed by laden with elegant youth; sumptuous galleys bore the ladies of the foremost families. Then came large peotes with the corporations, the brotherhoods and the companies each deploying its standard. The private gondolas competed in luxury. At the poop, silk trailed in the water; at the row, golden tritons and silver sires cleaved the waves with their swollen breasts. The sea carried floating flowerbeds of human flesh, which all came to incline before the victor of Lepanto, and feathers borne by the wind fluttered in the air like stamens.

A passing fisherman invited Dimitri into his boat. He leapt aboard and mingled with the movement of the festival, intoxicated by the sunlight, the colors and the music. When the *Bucentaur* had disembarked the senators and the hero of the day, the tide of boats began to ebb toward the Grand Canal.

The flood of high society had already gone by when Dimitri saw a gondola of a strange form arrive, which glided over the lagoon, svelte and rapid. The prow, raised up like a horse's head, and the poop, twisted in a dragon's tail, gave it the form of a sea-horse. A young woman in a pale blue dress, was lying limply rather than sitting in the boat. Her nacreous white neck emerged from a gray-green bodice sewn with silver flecks, like a siren emerging from the waves. Her head was the child-like and sensual type, essentially Venetian, that Veronese has given to Europe; vague desire and an immense curiosity of life pierced the timid veil of aristocratic modesty like a timid flash of lightning. Beneath the capricious forehead and the warm blonde curly tresses, a thousand frolicsome thoughts hid like a nest of young Amours about to take flight. Her eyes, the color of the sea, fixed themselves on Dmitri in passing with a vivid scintillation, but they only had time to brush him, for in the blink of a eye the gondola and the lady had disappeared behind the mole.

At that sight, under that gaze, Dimitri was dazzled, and felt throughout his being a commotion simultaneously painful and delectable. From that moment on, he no longer saw anything of the festival. He passed through his mind all the young women to whom he had talked in the evening on the banks of the canaletti, and all the women he had looked at from the corner of his eye as they passed by. None of them had produced that effect. Did the great ladies of Venice have the habit of casting spells on apprentice painters who had the audacity to gaze at them from the tip of the mole? It was im-

165

probable; and yet, whence came that gaze, and that impression?

He closed his eyes while the fisherman rowed him back to the Rialto. At first he experienced a great relief, but after a minute, strangely enough, the same scene as reproduced in his mind with a frightening exactitude. Again he saw the lagoon rippled by little wavelets, the gondola deigned in the distance, arriving as rapidly as the wind; the lady in the sparkling bodice smiled at him in passing; he felt a little flame running through him flowed by a frisson; then everything disappeared.

Twenty times Dimitri closed his eyes; it always returned. In the end, the return of the identical vision frightened him so much that he launched himself on to the bank and started running through the city.

Having arrived at Tintoretto's studio, Dimitri resumed a few sketches that were commenced. Fortunately, the siren and her sea-horse were effaced in a host of boats that cruised through the young painter's head like a confused phantasmagoria. He lay down, exhausted by fatigue and thought: *I'm cured!*

His eyes had been closed for a long time when it appeared to him that a woman clad in a somber garment came to stand at the foot of his bed. She resembled the lady in the gondola. Her eyes started shining and an aura shone around her head like those of Madonnas in churches. Her gaze seemed to be saying to Dimitri: "You will make my portrait. I want it."

Dimitri, who was not asleep, opened his eyes and sat up. The room was empty and the moonlight illuminated it fully. He lay down again, but without finding sleep. As soon as he closed his eyes, the lady was there.

For several days and nights Dimitri was persecuted by the same vision. In the end, he confided in the old gondolier in whose house he lived. Old Gianni knew all of Venice. He had served patricians and knew their habits. He started to laugh with a malign expression as he listened to the apprentice's story.

"Of course," he said, "I've seen her too. That's Nina Mocenigo, the widow of procurator Dolfini. She belongs by birth and her parents to the foremost families of Venice. If you obtain that lady's protection, your fortune is made. Listen! At present she goes to vespers every evening at the church of San Giovanni e Paolo. Try to talk to her. Who knows?"

Dimitri did not have to be told twice. At dusk, when the angelus rang, he posted himself behind one of the pillars in the church, near the exit, not far from the holy water font. Numerous unknown faces filed past. Finally, a brisk step made him shiver; a figure ached beneath a black mantle appeared in the doorway. But the lady was too well-veiled to be recognizable. She went to kneel at the back of the church. Dimitri did not budge; he was afraid of making a mistake, but he trembled all the more that it was her. When the crowd went out he looked at all the faces. The lady in the black mantle went past and dipped a white hand in the holy water without looking round.

The next day, there was the same performance, the same mute scene. Fortunately, however, a candle was burning next to the font and Dimitri perceived that the lady had deranged her veil slightly; a corner of her face was visible. He tottered with joy on recognizing the pretty siren of the festival of Lepanto. But she passed lightly and furtively, as she had the day before.

On the third evening, the noble lady, ever faithful to her vespers, arrived a little late. She came in slowly and approached the font cautiously. That evening, the pale

Nina was wearing a transparent veil, through which all her features were visible. Dimitri, pressed against the pillar, gazed at her ardently. As she took the holy water she attached a mild and curious gaze to him, appeared to hesitate, and resumed her route. The apprentice stayed nailed to the spot in anxious expectation until the end of the office. There was almost no one in the church when Nina went past again. She had removed her veil completely. Dimitri was emboldened to the point of offering her holy water with his fingertips.

"What is your name?" the lady murmured, in a familiar and tender voice.

"Dimitri."

"Your profession?"

"Painter, Excellency. I'm from Cyprus. I was sold here as a slave. Tintoretto adopted me. I work in his studio; I'm his pupil."

"And why do you come here every evening?"

"I come to hear vespers…and then, Signora I saw you at the festival of Lepanto. I was told that I could see you again here…and I came."

"It's said that you painters are great eccentrics," said the beautiful Nina, partly replacing her veil. "You, Dimitri, are a great child." Then, she added in a maternal tone, affecting to treat the young man as an adolescent: "And what can I be for you, *figliuolo mio*?"

Dimitri did not know how to respond to that question. He remained silent, and gazed at the aristocrat in mute adoration. She had a smile full of indulgence and grace. She contented herself with saying: "Think about it, my child."

And she left.

To tell the truth, Dimitri did not know what he expected from Nina Dolfini. Did she know what she was seeking in these furtive encounters? It is an exquisite pleasure, devoid of danger, to allow oneself to be adored by an ardent virgin who brings you the silent homage of his heart every day. And then, there was in the young painter's large Greek eyes a strength that the subtle noblewoman had not encountered elsewhere. She savored their charm, as a true daughter of Eve, but gradually, a certain emotion had overtaken her. For two days, she had not reappeared at San Giovanni e Paolo. Dimitri was beginning to despair.

On the third day, she returned, went straight to him, and gazed at him over the holy water font. Her siren charm had something irresistible that evening. Her eyes, the color of which varied between sea-green and azure, had a soft scintillation, and her smile a charming compassion.

"Well, Dimitri," she said, "have you nothing to ask me?"

Dimitri suddenly remembered Tintoretto's words and is own dream. He had a sudden inspiration and whispered quietly, in a passionate tone: "Oh, Signora, if I could paint your portrait!"

"Could you?" she said. And her gaze envelope Dimitri with an oblique caress in the dying light of the church.

"Yes, I sense it, I want it, I can!" cried Tintoretto's pupil, involuntarily animated. "Tomorrow I shall be alone, working in the church of Santa Maria dell'Orto. Come into the left-hand chapel at three o'clock. No one will disturb us, and I'll make a sketch of your ladyship!"

"In the church? A singular idea! Well, I'll be there."

That rapid dialogue had been stammered in low voices in a mysterious whisper, punctuated by silences and hesitations. Nina Dolfini replaced her veil and went out of the church with a light step, leaving Dimitri over-whelmed by joy and more astonished by his own bold-ness than the lady's unexpected confidence.

The little church of the Madonna dell'Orto, where Robusti's pupil had given his protectrice a rendezvous, was then, as it is today, one of the most modest and most solitary in Venice. Poor people have little time to give to their devotions, and Santa Maria dell'Orto was a poor church to the north-west of the city, in the popular quarter that was Tintoretto's quarter. The latter had been charged by the canon with executing a colossal painting of the Last Judgment for the choir. While the master was finishing it, Dimitri had obtained permission to spend all his afternoons in the church in order to copy a group of Saint Agnes. It is the painting that is still admired today in the grilled chapel to the left. Dimitri therefore dis-posed as the absolute master of that silent retreat, during the heavy hours that Venetians consecrate to the siesta, when even the sacristan slept the slumber of the blessed.

That day, Dimitri installed himself in the chapel at noon. He had brought a new canvas, sticks of charcoal and fresh colors. But, setting them aide, he resumed his daily task bravely, and set about modeling a crease in the robe of Saint Agnes. Twenty times he shifted his easel. The light disturbed him, his brushes were uncooperative and time very long.

Three o'clock chimed; the minutes became centu-ries. *She won't come now*, Dimitri thought, and he per-ceived that he had just made a large yellow patch on the saint's robe, when the rustle of a veritable robe informed him that someone was moving behind him. He turned round. Nina Dolfini was standing to his right, in a brown cape that allowed a very simple pale blue dress to be glimpsed. That discreet costume gave her a strange air of a woman of the people and a Madonna. The hood fell away of its own accord, and the smiling head, with its shining eyes and its aureole of blonde hair stood out against the gloom of the church.

"Well," she said, "are we going to commence the portrait?"

But Dmitri thought about his strange dream, the woman who said to him: "You will make my portrait. I want it." He saw the dazzling realization of it, and remained nonplussed.

"Oh, Madame," he said, finally, dropping the palette and the brush. "I would never dare!"

Nina was not annoyed by that weakness. She smiled, with a slight malice. "Poor child, you've been working too hard, haven't you? Rest for a while, and in the meantime, explain this painting to me."

Dimitri started to speak, boldly, about the miracle of Saint Agnes. He named the individuals in the painting and recounted the legend in simple and moving terms. From there he passed on to the intentions of the master, with such a warm vibration in his voice and such a poetic flame in his eyes that Nina felt touched by the sacred flame of art. She listened, astonished and pensive. The pupil was entirely reassured in gazing at his model. His initial anxiety had been succeeded by a sort of profound ecstasy produced by the presence and the smile of the beloved individual.

"Can I commence? I feel better now," he said with a sudden pride.

She sat down facing him; he began the sketch. Dimitri plunged to his work ardently, and Nina appeared to take a new pleasure in allowing the nascent painter to gaze at her fondly, for those eyes had the effluvia of a young Bacchus and the young Saint John.

Four o'clock chimed. Nina stood up anxiously.

"My cousin Loredani is visiting me at four o'clock, and if he divines that I've gone out...I'll no longer have any peace. Until tomorrow!"

She enveloped herself carefully in her mantle, traversed the church and regained her gondola.

Anyone other than Dimitri would have felt a sting at the name of the gentleman, which had just interrupted the dream of the child of the people. But what had Dimitri to do with cousin Loredani, and what did he know about the life of the opulent noblewoman? Had he not savored the presence of his Madonna for an hour? Had she not spoken the phrase full of promise: *until tomorrow?* What more did he need in order to be happy?

For a week the sittings continued in the discreet shade of the chapel. Dimitri, entirely devoted to his work, did not say much, and Nina only interrogated him with restraint. But gazes say a great deal when voices are silent. Their eyes often met, and the subtle flame that circulated between them excited the heart and soul of the young man more and more.

At the end of the week the widow came in with a feverish expression. Her gait and her face betrayed an unaccustomed agitation.

"Will you finish today?" she asked, anxiously.

"Yes, and you'll see my work!" exclaimed Tintoretto's pupil, who was not dreaming of anything beyond the moment when he would show the portrait to his model, as if, after that joy, the heavens would open for him and his Madonna.

She sat down in a sunbeam and gazed toward the window. A strange sadness gave her a more intense expression that day, and a sweeter charm. Dimitri had only to finish the eyes and the hair and give a few final touches to the face. At the moment when he picked up his palette, the organ of a nearby abbey began to play. It was a light sound, smooth and diaphanous, which seemed a melodious caress of the air. Was it an illusion of Dimitri's excited brain? It appeared to him that his model was transfigured and that her eyes took on an unexpected phosphorescence. The Madonna had become a woman, and her palpitating image revived the canvas. Rosy blood flowed under the caresses of the brush; the waves of blonde hair were gilded like an aureole, and the widened eyes were vibrant in a luminous fluid.

"She's alive!" Dimitri suddenly cried, dropping his palette and brush, his eyes fixed on his canvas.

Nina came running, looked, and smiled with joy on seeing herself. Her mirror had never sent her such a radiant image. Such was her delight that truly, at that moment, the model and the copy resembled one another.

"It's for me, isn't it?" she said.

"For you alone."

She became serious again, appeared to hesitate momentarily, and added: "Dimitri, it's necessary for us to say adieu. I'm leaving this evening for my country house on the edge of the Brenta."

"Forever?" stammered Dmitri, going pale. His eyes darkened. Nina was alarmed.

"No," she said. "I'll return in a month. You can bring me the portrait then. Come to my palace on the day of the Assumption; I'll recompense you."

"*Madonna mia!* I don't want any other recompense than to see you again!"

Those words were pronounced with a mixture of profound respect and ardent passion. Nina shivered. She saw Dimitri's eyes shining in the shadow, and felt his breath on her cheek. The lips of the imprudent noblewoman approached the painter's forehead. Lightly, almost without intending to, she imprinted a furtive kiss on that burning virgin forehead.

Dimitri closed his eyes and thought he might faint. He scarcely heard the murmured word: "*Addio!*" Then a mantle disappeared behind the grille; he was alone.

He no longer recognized himself. The blood was throbbing in his veins, flooding his head; he finally understood the force of amour. His senses, dazed by the ecstasy of the beautiful and the labor of the artist, awoke with a start under the fatal kiss. He shook his easel furiously. He threw himself on the chair that Nina had just quit, and tried to embrace hr vanished form. But she had only left him a burn on the forehead and her adieu, which was still floating in the air with the perfume of her hair.

IV

The next day, Tintoretto said to his pupil: "Signor Maffeo Barbarello told me yesterday that he wants a portrait by you. You'll go this morning. Try to do well; Barbarello is very influential in Venice.

"I'll go, Master, and I'll do my best," Dimitri replied, pensively. All occupations had been indifferent to him since he was no longer going to the church of Santa Maria dell'Orto.

The Duke of Ferrara's envoy lived on the Grand Canal on the first floor of a magnificent palace. Dimitri went up a marble staircase and penetrated into a vast and splendid paneled hall. A gracious disorder was visible there in all the objects that the gentlemen of the Renaissance loved to put on display: amphorae, Murano crystal, gold and silver vases, swords, antique medals, and richly bound books ornamented with arabesques. At the back, the entrance to an alcove was discernible, sustained by caryatids. The room was full of a joyous company of artists, scholars and young lords, all in the process of paying their court to the Duke of Ferrara's envoy, who, thanks to his master, his fortune and his accomplished manners, set the tone for the gilded youth of Venice.

Sitting in a gilded leather armchair, Maffeo was chatting to two poets and negligently plucking a mandolin with his beautiful hand—which did not prevent his sculpted dagger from glinting strangely over his violet velvet doublet, any less than his steel gray eyes and the brilliant locks of his chestnut-colored hair.

Loredani was conversing gallantly with Veronica Franco, a celebrated courtesan who had been Titian's mistress and had quarreled with the great master, already old, since the latter had fallen madly in love with a daughter of Palma. Now Veronica kept house, receiving the artistic elite in her home. The great foreign lords that she went to visit during her morning excursions received her on a footing of equality. The beautiful brunette with the masculine gaze, whose torso of a bacchante emerged from a marten fur as from a nebris, was in the process of delivering a slightly humorous commentary on some verses by Ovid that a scholar was reciting in a loud voice, and which Loredani, who prided himself on his Latin, was translating into Italian. The three nurses of the Muses frequently irrigated their studies with wine of Imola, which they were drinking from nacre cups mounted on pink coral branches, the handles of which were little silver Amours or Nereids.

Dimitri place his canvas on his easel and began sketching.

"You'll paint me thus, with my mandolin," said Maffeo, "like one of Tasso's shepherds; for I love pastoral poetry, my lords."

The poets bowed.

"Have you heard the news?" Veronica said, suddenly, raising her voice. "I know a little more about the secrets of Venice than you do, Signor Barbarello. Know, then that Loredani is soon going to marry Nina Dolfini, nicknamed since the festival the Siren of Lepanto.

Dimitri broke a stick of charcoal. A group of poets and painters surrounded Loredani in order to congratulate him.

"A fine marriage!" they said, in chorus.

"Thank you, my friends," said Loredani, slightly embarrassed. "Except that there isn't a word of truth in what you've just heard."

"Truly?" said Veronica. "How is it then, that in all the companies, theaters and regattas you're seen so urgent around the young widow? At the tourneys in the Plaza San Marco, you don't take your eyes off her. On the lagoon your gondola is always behind hers, and at the festival of Murano you fluttered around her all evening?"

"She's my distant cousin. I'm doing my duty as a relative."

"That's true. It's claimed that the late and regretted procurator of the Republic. Taddeo Dolfini, appointed you his widow's guardian in his testament. You're filling that role with an admirable devotion. But it's said that the poor thing is sighing for her liberty and that you're prolonging the yoke of marriage for her. You've assumed a terrible responsibility. But courage, Signor Loredani; you're the Doge's cousin and you know Latin. With that, it's necessary not to despair of anything."

"It's permitted for you to laugh at the mores of our great Venetian families," said Loredani, with a disdainful smile, "which are more severe than those of the rest of Italy. I don't know who will marry my cousin, but what I can affirm is that the blood of the Loredanis that flows in her veins will not permit the slightest stain on its blazon."

Having said that, Loredani took his leave of the company, with a group of lords and artists. Veronica stood up and leaned over Maffeo's shoulder with a malicious smile.

"Did you notice," she said, "that Loredani put his toque on backwards? He only ever does that when he's annoyed."

"You think he's in love with his cousin?"

"I'm sure of it."

"And what is this Nina Dolfini, then?" said Maffeo, without quitting his attitude of an impassive observer.

"A flower of the lagoon, but what a flower!" replied a young man who wore a tuft of his own blond hair like a crest for his toque. "Eve going to pick her apple; Pandora opening her box and Psyche holding her lamp, didn't have a more enchanting smile. It's the innocence that plays with sin, the charm that interrogates and doubts itself."

"The portrait is flattering," said Veronica,

"It's exact," said Maffeo.

"You know her, then?"

"Slightly; and I hope to know her even better," replied Maffeo, whose impenetrable gray eyes lit up with a strange gleam.

"Good!" concluded Veronica Franco, laughing. "I finally recognize you Barbarello. Are we not both from Ferrara, which has the motto: *Victory to the boldest*? Good luck, Maffeo, and *au revoir*."

Maffeo accompanied Veronica as far as her gondola, and through the window Dimitri heard their laughter and their sallies repeated in the sonorous echoers of the Grand Canal.

When he returned, Barbarello dismissed the painter and told him to come back the next day. Dimitri had not understood the implications of the conversation, but it had riddled him with pin-pricks and chilled his heart. He went home deeply upset. The audacity of Veronica Franco, the impertinence of all the young lords and the indecipherable smile of the handsome Maffeo made him quiver with indignation and a vague dread.

Was the Nina Dolfini of whom they dared to speak so lightly really the ravishing Madonna who had come to the chapel of Santa Maria dell'Orto for him and had posed that mysterious kiss on his forehead like a seal of love and fidelity? No; that was not possible, or rather, those who spoke thus did not know her. Dimitri ran upstairs to his bedroom, where he had hidden the portrait of Nina. He looked at it, and felt completely reassured. Could those eyes lie?

V

When Tintoretto's pupil returned to Maffeo Barbarello's house in the days that followed he found him alone, and never heard him pronounce Nina's name again. His heart was relieved by that; but another circumstance soon reawakened all his anxieties. One evening when he was passing along the Grand Canal in a gondola with Gianni, he was astonished to see the Dolfini palace brightly illuminated. He learned from the gondoliers stationed outside that the widow was giving a great fête. She had not, therefore, gone to the country, as she had told him!

The arched windows stood out like black lace against the illuminated background; the silhouettes of men and women wandered over the balcony. Dimitri felt himself suffocating. He asked Gianni to take him to the lagoon. A great wind was raising abrupt waves there; the sea could be heard howling on the far side of the Lido, and the distant roar had something sinister about it.

The orphan suddenly thought about his island, Cyprus, and the nights of the Orient. He felt more alone than ever, and his second fatherland, Tintoretto's studio, was no longer sufficient for him. Then, from the black depths of the sea, the fascinating image of the Siren returned to him. Doubts, fears and suffering, all his sensations and all his thoughts sunk as if in whirlpool in a single idea: in a week, I shall see her again!

A forceful shock, followed by a cry from Gianni, wrenched him from his reverie. One of the gusts of wind that the gondoliers call *ruffolo*, which are very dangerous for small boats, had caught the gondola side-on and threatened to capsize it. Dimitri remained bleak and indifferent to the peril. The storm drove the boat into the canal of the Giudecca, and Gianni, curing and swearing, brought his guest back to the house; the latter's heart, less fortunate than the gondola, continue to be tossed and tormented all night long by a tempest more formidable than the one outside.

It was in a state of increasing fever that Dimitri saw the day of the Assumption approaching on which, according to Nina's instruction, he ought to bring her the portrait. He only breathed for that moment; five or six days still separated him from it.

One evening, Gianni said to Dimitri: "The Duke of Gonzaga is giving a masked ball tonight in the gardens of Murano. Get the costume of page and a mask from Tintoretto's studio. Tell the gardener of the villa that you've come on my behalf. He'll let you in and you'll see the fête. Would you like that?"

Dimitri accepted. Anything seemed good to him in order to forget his thoughts. That night, Gianni was in service at the Traghetto. Dimitri, costumed as a page and enveloped in a large cloak, set out alone for Murano in a small boat that was easy to manipulate. When he landed on the island he confided his boat to a gondolier and introduced himself to the gardener of the duke's villa. Thanks to Gianni's name, the latter, with the fine manner and pretty costume of a young man, let him into the splendid gardens, brightly illuminated by thousands of girandoles, through a little door.

The clump of cork-oaks formed arbors there ornamented with statues and fountains. Mysterious couples were strolling in the long pathways; others were dancing to the sound of a invisible orchestra on laws bordered by the foliage of acanthus and moss-roses. But all those unknown people, those ironic and searching eyes behind black masks, made Dimitri anxious. He took refuge in a deserted spot at the extremity of the garden. That wooded peninsula advanced into the lagoon and terminated in a terrace. A statue of Flora was discreetly hidden there under a grove of green oaks. Seen from there, Venice, with its steeples and campaniles, resembled a somber fleet asleep on the sea.

Dimitri scarcely had time to admire that landscape, for laughing voices, a man's and a woman's, approached. They seemed familiar to him. He was afraid and he hid in the trees.

Loredani, in the most elegant costume of the Calza, a red simarre and a blue doublet, holding his pink mask in his hand, appeared with a masked woman clad in black velvet. They sat down on a marble bench under the statue of Flora, and Dimitri overheard heir conversation.

"To what god or goddess do I owe the honor, beautiful cousin, of being brought by you to this solitary place?"

"To Flora here, handsome cousin. Solitude pleases me this evening."

"You, who can only live surrounded by dancing, music and fashionable cavaliers?"

"What about this perfumed boscage, that tranquil sea and the wind sighing in the crowns of the cypresses? What could be more delightful?"

"Yes, beautiful cousin, since you are here. And now that we're alone…you'll listen to me…"

"Hush! I'm going to close your mouth with my fan."

"I tell you that you'll listen to me!"

"Not this evening; tomorrow."

"You've been saying that to me for six months."

"Well, wait six more and perhaps I'll tell you to speak."

"Another six months? For as many, I've been the humblest of servant cavaliers without obtaining any other response than that. And what I'm asking of you is the simplest thing in the world, the most honest and the sagest: a promise of marriage."

"And when I've given it, will I be forced to keep it?"

"Oh, as to that—yes!"

"Well then, let me think about it a little longer."

"If marriage frightens you so much…well, let's talk about love! Do you remember one evening…on the edge of your balcony…"

"Hush! Shut up! Rather finish telling me the story of that strange man, that adventurer you were talking about a little while ago. What was his name?"

"Maffeo Barbarello? He's truly not worth the trouble. The costume of a lord, the manners of a condottiere and the heart of a spy. He cheats at cards and wears a breastplate under his doubt because he's afraid that someone will return the thrusts of the stiletto he's delivered. He kills husbands who inconvenience him and poisons women who weary him. In Rome he seduced a marquise, and was ordered by the Pope to marry the lady. What did Maffeo do? He had her put in prison by order of the Holy Office on a charge of heresy. Isn't that gallant?"

"What a monster! But go on."

"He interests you greatly, then?"

"I'm horrified by him. But what does he look like?"

"Like a demon without a soul. He only has one merit: his voice."

At that moment, one of the boats illuminated boats known as galleggiante, which carry serenades, passed some distance from the shore. A harp and a viol vibrated. Then a profound and voluptuous baritone voice modulated a Sicilian song. The ardent melody rose up to burst like a flower of light; then, slowly, it allowed its petals to fall back languidly in dying notes into the warm night. The silence that followed seemed to be impregnated with fire,

The masked woman had shuddered. After a moment, she said to her companion: "You were talking about beautiful voices; what do you say to that one? Isn't it marvelous?"

"Yes," said Loredani, anxiously, "but the music's no good. Let's go. Is there anything more stupid than the lagoon?"

"Yes, let's go. My gondola's waiting for me; you go and rejoin the duke, who wants to introduce you to a first-rate Latinist."

"Why, beautiful cousin, are you extinguishing that poor lantern burning at Flora's feet?"

"It has burned for us, and I don't want it to burn for others."

"Always crazy!" aid Loredani; and he attempted to kiss his cousin through the mask. She responded with a thrust of her fan and slipped through his hands.

The voices fell silent, the footsteps died away. The couple had disappeared into Flora's grove.

"She doesn't love him!" Dimitri exclaimed, with the instinct of amour. "She doesn't love him! What joy!" And he launched himself out of the clump of bushes.

Then he perceived the illuminated boat, still motionless. A gondola that was following it turned on itself and came to touch the terrace. A man leapt on to the shore and searched the boscage with his eyes. Dimitri went back into his hiding place. He was greatly astonished to see the masked woman returning at a furtive pace. Was it really the same one?

The cavalier approached her, took her hand and whispered: "This evening..."

"And forever," the woman replied.

"You recognized my voice?"

"You saw the lantern go out?"

"A fortunate signal. My gondola is here. Quickly! I hear noises."

The man and the woman slid under the *fels*, and the gondola departed like an arrow.

Dimitri had passed from a mad joy to a sharp dolor. His head spun. He could not doubt that the masked woman who had been talking to Loredani was Nina Dolfini But the one who, perfidiously and audaciously, had thrown herself into the arms of the unknown singer, was that the same one? Was that the Madonna of Santa Maria dell'Orto?

Impossible, Dimitri thought. *If I had only seen her face! If I could follow her! But what can I do?*

He emerged from the garden, ran to the marina, threw himself into the miserable fishing boat in which he had come set forth after the accursed gondola. It was still following the boat that carried the serenade, drawn by that enchanting music on the wings of the wind. Dmitri had great difficulty following at a distance the light skiff that two vigorous gondoliers were causing to fly over the water. He rowed forcefully, but the gondola was traveling more rapidly, and the viol was singing and the oboe uttering its sights. He bent over the oars and stiffened his arms, but the gondola was far away, and in the gusts of the sirocco, the poor rower thought he could hear stifled laughter and kisses...

Out of breath, Dimitri's head was on fire and his oars were now only striking with desperate thrusts. Finally, the serenade and the gondola reached Venice. Guided by the lanterns and the sound of instruments that were only playing softly now, Dimitri pursued them into a tortuous labyrinth of small black canals. Soon, the galleggiante and its musicians disappeared and the gondola stopped in a very dark place. When Dimitri reached it, the lovers' boat had already disappeared into a sort of cellar, and a low door of the palace, situated at water level, closed discreetly upon them.

Dimitri found himself alone in the moonlight, in the solitude of the canaletto. Only then did he perceive that the palace was the one in which Maffeo Barbarello occupied the first floor. The façade overlooked the Grand Canal, the side overlooked one of the narrow canals that Venice encased between tall buildings, and which have something mysterious and lugubrious about them by night.

"Maffeo Barbarello! So it's him!" stammered the apprentice; and he ran his eyes over the somber walls of the edifice. A profound silence reigned therein; not a single window was illuminated. Dimitri felt something within him that told him to flee, but an invisible force held him chained to the foot of the palace where his tortures had commenced. *L'occhio non vede, il cuore non duole,*[11] says the Italian proverb. Tintoretto's pupil had, however seen and heard enough to suffer horribly. But he had not seen the woman's face; what if it were not her? That hope kept coming back to him.

---

[11] What the eye does not see, the heart does not grieve over.

Exhausted by fatigue, streaming with sweat, he sat down facing the palace on the steps of a little stairway that rose up to a deserted back street. He let his burning head fall into his hands and started thinking. He remained thus for a long time, without perceiving that his feet were in the water. Was all this not a bad dream?

At that moment, a ray of moonlight fell directly into the narrow canaletto and illuminated a row of houses. Dimitri was hidden in dense shadow, in the angle of the wall. He raised his head. Opposite him, a window giving access to a small balcony had opened. A man and a woman were leaning on the stone balustrade. It really was Maffeo. The woman, without a domino and bare-shouldered, was wearing a white satin dress, but she still had her mask on, and, leaning over the balcony, she seemed to be sounding the depths of the canaletto with her gaze, in order to see whether it was completely deserted.

Maffeo drew nearer to the lady and spoke to her in a low voice. Then, slowly, gently, the woman raised her hand to her mask and removed it. Dimitri, standing up and craning his neck, felt a cold blade traverse his heart on recognizing the face of Nina Dolfini, bathed with a soft languor in the moonlight, and as pale as a nenuphar emerging from the water.

Maffeo drew her into his arms; she folded like a water-plant, and, her head tilted back and her lips parted, fell on to her lover's shoulder...

Dmitri uttered a stifled cry, tottered, and fell into the canal, as stiff as a plank.

VI

The next morning, Tintoretto, having risen at dawn, was standing in his studio. The great canvas of the Last Judgment, which was to be the glory of his parish church of Santa Maria dell'Orto, was only lacking the topmost part: the sky. Placed at the bottom of the scaffolding, the master was now casting a gaze of satisfaction over the ensemble his work.

In that strange and bold conception, he had wanted to represent all the degrees of transformation of human flesh at the moment of resurrection. At the bottom, nature was surprised in a new labor of birth; from the earth, from the waters, dubious forms were surging. Semi-reanimated cadavers were floating on the pale waters; skeletons were emerging from tombs and being reclad in flesh. In the semi-darkness, lovers brilliant with immortal youth were launching themselves toward one another and recognizing one another, astonished. One might have thought that at the trumpet of judgment, a new fury of life and creation has taken possession of nature.

To the left, Saint Michael was precipitating into Hell a human avalanche that had tried to force the gates of Heaven; but to the right, charming floating forms rising into the air on an azure clarity made one things of human souls which, above the enchainment of blind forces, aspiring to the divine light of consciousness and amour.

Robusti enjoyed his work now, embracing it with a single glance. His eagle eyes rolled powerfully beneath his broad, protruding forehead furrowed by numerous lateral wrinkles. It was as if the impetuous imagination were purified and appeased in rising toward superior spheres. He got ready to paint the Christ as the judge of Heaven and earth.

The door opened abruptly, and Gianni came in tremulously. The master, absorbed in his meditation, did not take his eyes off his painting. The gondolier seized his arm.

"Well, what is it?"

"A misfortune, Master," Gianni stammered. "Dimitri...fell into a canaletto last night. A passing gondolier fished him out and brought him back to my house. We brought him round, but he has a terrible fever."

"Dimitri?" said the master, only half-understanding. "Why did he fall into a canaletto?"

"I don't know," replied Gianni, who felt slightly responsible for the accident, "but what is certain is that he's very ill."

"Dimitri! The son of my soul!" cried Tintoretto, finally awoken from his dream.

Robusti dropped his palette and followed Gianni to his house. Dimitri was in bed. The gondolier's wife and son were caring for him. Sometimes as white as a sheet, he trembled with fever, sometimes crimson, he entered into delirium and only spoke incoherent words. Robusti believed it to be an artistic despair. Like all men of genius, Tintoretto lived absorbed in his work, and like the majority of them, he tyrannized his entourage somewhat; but beneath his brusque and ironic manner hid an ardent soul and a profound sensibility. Dimitri, the lost child of the isles, the redeemed slave that he wanted to make the heir of his genius, had captured the best of his soul. Robusti reproached himself for having neglected him. Somber, his head bowed, the master remained seated at the beside of the moribund pupil. When Dimitri's eyes opened, they seemed to be full of an immense anger against an invisible object. Tintoretto did not understand; he only divined one thing, which was that his adoptive son had tried to commit suicide.

He spent three days and three nights with the invalid. But his efforts and those of the physician were futile. Dimitri's strength was diminishing by the hour, without him emerging from the delirium for a single instant. However, as he became weaker, he appeared to return to himself. On the morning after the third night his eyes recovered their lucidity.

"Dimitri, my dear child," said Tintoretto, "Why did you want to kill yourself?"

Dimitri looked at Robusti fondly, with a strange penetration.

"Master," he said, in an almost extinct voice, "you told me that I would be a true painter if I were able to make the portrait of the woman I loved. She came to Santa Maria dell'Orto. The painting is over there."

Tintoretto went to take a canvas from a corner of the room, which he turned around and studied. It was the head of a woman of an insinuating charm and a marvelous life, which stood out against a dark background, bathed in undulating hair as if in a golden fluid. The lost eyes were swimming in an amorous ecstasy.

Sitting up in his bed, Dimitri also looked at the portrait and murmured: "There she is! It's her! She's come back…Madonna mia!"

Stupefied, Robusti could not take his eyes off the canvas. Suddenly, he turned round, exclaiming: "Dimitri! Dimitri! I wasn't wrong! You're a great painter!"

And the transported master hugged the child in his muscular arms. Dimitri was still gazing at the portrait placed in front of him at the end of the bed. His eyes were radiant. Suddenly, his head fell back on Tintoretto's arm; his gaze was extinguished. The face became the color of wax, and then the color of ash. The pupil, lost in a dream, had died without even hearing his consecration by his master's mouth.

VII

One morning, Nina Dolfini awake fresh and rosy in her boudoir hung with white satin spangled with silver. She placed her dainty feet on a blood red Turkish carpet varied with pale pink streaks, and went to sit down in front of her mirror. She had slept for a long time; it was nearly midday and the façades of the palaces were dazzlingly white with their Moorish ogives, their colonnades of porphyry and serpentine, reflected joyously in the glaucous waters of the Grand Canal. The sunlight was cheerful, and Nina was even more cheerful. The eyes of the nereid were shining with bright gleams, like the water of the canaletto, the reflection of which, filtered by the blinds, was trembling on the painted ceiling of the boudoir.

"What day is it?" she asked Rizetta, who had just brought her a bouquet of flowers from the terra firma—the great luxury of Venice—on behalf of Signor Maffeo Barbarello.

"Yesterday was the day of the Assumption," said the chambermaid.

Nina had completely forgotten Dimitri in the turbulence of her new life, but she recalled that the young painter had promised to bring her portrait to her on the day of the Assumption, and that day had passed.

"Didn't Tintoretto's pupil come yesterday?"

"No, Signora."

"That's singular."

Nina Dolfini easily forgot others, but she did not like to be forgotten. The apprentice's inexactitude piqued her. She desired that portrait keenly. Then, the memory of the large dark eyes that looked fondly at her with such a pure flame had something sweet and reassuring for her at that moment. Why were they no longer there? She felt gripped by a violent whim, an anxious need to see them again. But how could she find Dimitri? She did not know where he lived. Perhaps he would be at the church where he had the habit of working.

She asked for her gondola, and in spite of the heat of the day she went to Santa Maria dell'Orto.

The place was solitary and the church was deserted, as usual. When she went in she saw a catafalque set up in the choir, which appeared to be awaiting the mass for the dead. A frisson gripped her. She took a few steps, looking for Dimitri; the chapel was empty. But in the nave a middle-aged man who hair was already graying was standing with his arms folded and his eyes fixed on the catafalque. At the sound of footsteps on the paving stones he turned round. She did not know him, but he appeared to recognize her...and his eyes blazed. She was afraid and she stopped, fascinated.

"Who are you looking for here?" said the man with the severe face.

"Isn't this where Dmitri, Tintoretto's pupil, works?"

"It's here that he worked, yes; but he's no longer working. He's dead."

Nina went as white as candle-wax.

"Dimitri? Dead? Him? But a month ago I saw him flourishing, full of life."

"Dimitri was in love. He died of the fever of amour."

The young woman, tottering, leaned on a pillar.

"When did he die?"

"Two days ago."

"He's being buried?"

"Today."

"Where is he?"

"There, in that coffin. And I, Madame, am his master, Tintoretto."

Nina trembled as if before the judge of the last judgment, and felt herself fainting. She slid to her knees on the flagstones and covered her face with her hands. Robusti did not make any move to retain her, and looked at her silently, his arms still folded. She remained immobile or a long time.

Finally, she stammered: "Master…I want to accompany your pupil to the cemetery."

"Why? That child was everything for me; what was he for you?"

"Not even that? Master, you're cruel! Not even a memory of him? The portrait! In order to have that, I'd give all that I possess."

"All the gold in your palace wouldn't be sufficient. That portrait is the only thing that remains of him; it's mine. Oh, Siren, you have killed that child, who would have been a great painter, and you want to steal the flower of his genius from me? No, you shall not have it. You don't know what the soul was that he had given to you, If you can ever comprehend, come to weep over his tomb, but not before. Woman, your place is not in the sanctuary of grief. Return to the world from which you came and leave me to bury the son of my soul."

Under that condemnation, the noblewoman recovered her pride momentarily and stood up, quivering; but she could not articulate a word, or sustain the gaze of her judge, who showed her the open door of the church with a gesture. She went out, seized by vertigo, without seeing anything except a large black patch floating before her eyes. That patch had the form of a catafalque and was interposed between her and the blinding daylight.

Having reached her gondola she finally collected herself and breathed. At the movement of the boat, which glided, rocking gently, under the August sun, she tried to chase away the funereal vision by means of more cheerful images. But then a voice from the depths of her being rose up and said to her;

"The amour that sleeps under that black sheet you will not find again—never again."

Tintoretto and the gondolier's family conducted Dimitri's corpse to the cemetery. On returning, the master shut himself away in his studio and stayed there for a long time without picking up his brushes; but when the gleams of the setting sun came to turn the top of the immense canvas crimson, he climbed up on the scaffold in order to paint the head of his Christ.

ALSO FROM BLACK COAT PRESS

( ) Charles de Fieux, Chevalier de Mouhy. Lamekis

( ) Judith Gautier: Isoline and the Serpent-Flower

( ) Jules Janin. The Magnetized Corpse

( ) Gustave Kahn. The Tale of Gold and Silence

( ) Paul Lacroix. Danse Macabre

( ) Louis-Guillaume de La Follie. The Unpretentious Philosopher

( ) Etienne-Léon de Lamothe-Langon. The Virgin Vampire

( ) Etienne-Léon de Lamothe-Langon. The Mysterious Hermit of the Tomb

( ) Maurice Level. The Gates of Hell

( ) Marie-Jeanne L'Héritier de Villandon. The Robe of Sincerity

( ) André Lichtenberger. The Centaurs

( ) André Lichtenberger. The Children of the Crab

( ) Monsieur de Listonai. The Philosophical Voyager

( ) Jean-Marc & Randy Lofficier. The French Fantasy Treasury (Vol. 1) (anthology)

( ) Jean-Marc & Randy Lofficier. The French Fantasy Treasury (Vol. 2) (anthology)

( ) Jean-Marc & Randy Lofficier. The French Fantasy Treasury (Vol. 3) (anthology)

( ) Charles Lomon & P.-B. Gheusi. The Last Days of Atlantis

( ) Marie-Madeleine de Lubert. Princess Camion

( ) Charles Malato. Lost!

( ) Maurice Magre. The Marvelous Story of Claire d'Amour

( ) Maurice Magre. The Call of the Beast

( ) Maurice Magre. Priscilla of Alexandria

( ) Maurice Magre. The Angel of Lust

( ) Maurice Magre. The Mystery of the Tiger

( ) Maurice Magre. The Poison of Goa

( ) Maurice Magre. Lucifer

( ) Maurice Magre. The Blood of Toulouse

( ) Maurice Magre. The Albigensian Treasure

( ) Maurice Magre. Jean de Fodoas

( ) Maurice Magre. Melusine

( ) Maurice Magre. The Brothers of the Virgin Gold

( ) Catulle Mendes. The Little Fays in the Air
( ) Louis-Sébastien Mercier. The Iron Man
( ) Joseph Méry. The Tower of Destiny
( ) Hippolyte Mettais. Paris Before the Deluge
( ) Henriette-Julie de Murat. The Palace of Vengeance
( ) Marie Nizet. Captain Vampire
( ) Charles Nodier. Trilby   The Crumb Fairy
( ) Pierre-Alexis Ponson du Terrail. The Vampire and the Devil's Son
( ) Pierre-Alexis Ponson du Terrail. The Immortal Woman
( ) Pierre-Alexis Ponson du Terrail. The Police Agent
( ) Edgar Quinet. Ahasuerus
( ) Edgar Quinet. The Enchanter Merlin
( ) Restif de la Bretonne. Discovery of the Austral Continent
( ) Restif de la Bretonne. Posthumous Correspondence (Vol. 1)
( ) Restif de la Bretonne. Posthumous Correspondence (Vol. 2)
( ) Restif de la Bretonne. Posthumous Correspondence (Vol. 3)
( ) Restif de la Bretonne. Posthumous Correspondence (all 3 volumes)
( ) Restif de la Bretonne. The Story of the Great Prince Oribeau (The Fay Ouroucoucou 1)
( ) Restif de la Bretonne. The Four Beauties and the Four Beasts (The Fay Ouroucoucou 2)
( ) Marie-Anne de Roumier-Robert. The Voyages of Lord Seaton to the Seven Planets
( ) Louis-Claude de Saint-Martin. The Crocodile
( ) Nicolas Segur. The Human Paradise
( ) Nicolas Segur. Penelope's Secret
( ) Pierre de Sélènes. An Unknown World
( ) Brian Stableford. News from the Moon (anthology)
( ) Brian Stableford. The Germans on Venus (anthology)
( ) Brian Stableford. The Supreme Progress (anthology)
( ) Brian Stableford. The World Above the World (anthology)
( ) Brian Stableford. Nemoville (anthology)
( ) Brian Stableford. Investigations of the Future (anthology)
( ) Brian Stableford. The Conqueror of Death (anthology)
( ) Brian Stableford. The Revolt of the Machines (anthology)

( ) Brian Stableford. The Man With the Blue Face (anthology)
( ) Brian Stableford. The Aerial Valley (anthology)
( ) Brian Stableford. The New Moon (anthology)
( ) Brian Stableford. The Nickel Man (anthology)
( ) Brian Stableford. On the Brink of the Worl's End (anthology)
( ) Brian Stableford. The Mirror of Present Events (anthology)
( ) Brian Stableford. The Humanisphere (anthology)
( ) Brian Stableford. Journey to the Isles of Atlantis (anthology)
( ) Brian Stableford. The Queen of the Fays (anthology)
( ) Brian Stableford. Funestine (anthology)
( ) Brian Stableford. The Origin of the Fays (anthology)
( ) Brian Stableford. Tales of Enchantment and Disenchantment (anthology + non-fiction)
( ) Charles-François Tiphaigne de La Roche. Amilec
( ) Simon Tyssot de Patot. The Strange Voyages of Jacques Massé and Pierre de Mésange
( ) Louis Ulbach. Prince Bonifacio
( ) Villiers de l'Isle-Adam. The Scaffold
( ) Villiers de l'Isle-Adam. The Vampire Soul
( ) Willy. Astral Amour

www.ingramcontent.com/pod-product-compliance
Lightning Source LLC
Chambersburg PA
CBHW060400030726
47497CB00003B/793